## *Will the Tanner sisters strike a pose at the big modeling contest—or strike out?*

### STEPHANIE

Competing in the Sisters Modeling Contest with Michelle will be so much fun! Stephanie can't wait to walk the catwalk! But she may never get her chance—because Michelle is nowhere to be found!

If she doesn't show up soon, the sisters will be disqualified from the contest—and Stephanie's modeling dreams will be down the drain.

Where in the world could Michelle be?

### MICHELLE

A secret job at the mall was supposed to be a fun way for Michelle to earn extra money—money to buy Stephanie a surprise birthday present.

But Stephanie entered Michelle in the Sisters Modeling Contest—and Michelle's supposed to be modeling at the same time she's working at her secret job! If Michelle misses her job, she won't be able to buy Stephanie's present—and if she misses the contest, she and Stephanie will be disqualified!

How will Michelle get out of this jam?

**FULL HOUSE™: SISTERS books**

Two on the Town
One Boss Too Many
And the Winner Is . . .

Available from MINSTREL Books

# FULL HOUSE™
## Sisters

### And the Winner Is . . .

### NINA ALEXANDER

A Parachute Book

A MINSTREL® BOOK

Published by POCKET BOOKS
New York   London   Toronto   Sydney   Tokyo   Singapore

A MINSTREL PAPERBACK *Original*

A Minstrel Book published by
POCKET BOOKS, a division of Simon & Schuster Inc.
1230 Avenue of the Americas, New York, NY 10020

A PARACHUTE BOOK

Copyright © and ™ 1999 by Warner Bros.

ISBN: 0-671-04055-3

First Minstrel Books printing October 1999

10  9  8  7  6  5  4  3  2  1

A MINSTREL BOOK and colophon are registered trademarks of Simon & Schuster Inc.

Cover photo by Schultz Photography

Printed in the U.S.A.

# STEPHANIE

# Chapter
# 1

Eight A.M.?" Stephanie Tanner moaned. She brushed her long blond hair out of her eyes and stared at the buzzing alarm clock on her bedside table. "It's Saturday. What was I *thinking?*" She hit the button to stop the alarm.

Her best friend, Allie Taylor, sat up in her sleeping bag and yawned. She rubbed her eyes. "You were thinking we needed to get up early so we could get to the new mall right when it opens. Remember?"

"Oh, right." Stephanie glanced over at Michelle's bed on the side of the room. The bed was empty, which meant that Stephanie's ten-year-old sister was up already. She leaned over the other side of her bed and poked her other best friend, Darcy Powell, on the shoulder.

Darcy groaned and turned over in her sleeping bag. "What time is it?" she croaked, keeping her dark brown eyes shut tight.

"Time to hit the mall," Stephanie answered. "Rise and shine!"

Darcy groaned again and pulled the top of her sleeping bag over her head. Stephanie and Allie grinned at each other. Darcy was high-energy when she was awake, but sometimes it took her a while to get that way.

"Come on, Darce," Allie said. "Don't you want to be there to meet Fiona and Felicia Miarra?"

"I can't believe that the Miarras are opening a boutique here in San Francisco," Stephanie said. "It's so cool!"

"And they'll actually be here for the next two weeks," Darcy added. "Imagine walking through the mall and meeting two of the most famous fashion designers in the world!"

Allie stretched her arms and yawned. "Just

because they're opening a new boutique here doesn't mean they'll be walking around the mall with the rest of us."

"You never know." Stephanie tossed her pillow at Allie. "And just in case they *are* there, we'd better make sure we look awesome. Who knows? Maybe they'll decide to put us in their next big fashion show in Paris!" She wiggled her eyebrows up and down and smiled.

"Yeah, right," Allie said. Then she sniffed the air. "Mmm, I smell pancakes."

"Yum," Darcy stood up. "I love your dad's pancakes. Let's go get some!"

The three friends hurried down the stairs of Stephanie's big Victorian-style house and headed straight for the kitchen. They found the rest of the family gathered around the big wooden table. Stephanie and her friends took their seats at the table.

"Morning, everyone," Stephanie said cheerfully. She glanced around at the eight other people in her family.

Her family wasn't exactly what you'd call *typical*, but Stephanie kind of liked it that way.

Aside from Stephanie and Michelle, there was her dad, Danny, and her nineteen-year-old sister, D.J.

Danny's best friend, Joey, and his brother-in-law, Jesse, moved in almost nine years ago to help out when Stephanie's mother died. Then Jesse married Becky. Later the two of them had twins, Nicky and Alex. Now they lived in the attic apartment.

All together, they were nine people and one large golden retriever named Comet under one roof. Sometimes, the full house drove Stephanie crazy. But most of the time, she knew she wouldn't want to live any other way.

D.J. glanced up from her pancakes. "Why are you guys awake so early on a Saturday?" she asked.

"Yeah. What's the occasion?" Danny turned away from the stove and headed to the table, carrying a platter piled high with golden pancakes. "You three usually snooze until noon after one of your sleepovers."

"Get with it, Danny," Joey said playfully. "They haven't even gone to sleep yet. They're just coming down for an eight A.M. snack."

4

Stephanie smiled. "Come on, stop kidding around," she told her family. "You know the new mall opens today. I've been talking about it all week."

"Oh, is that this weekend?" Danny set the pancakes on the table and smacked his forehead. "I'm sorry, Steph. I totally forgot. I can't drive you there. I made other plans."

"What?" Stephanie gasped. "But, Dad, you promised!"

Michelle quickly covered her mouth with a hand, her face turning red.

Stephanie crossed her arms over her chest. Then she eyed the rest of her family. They stared at her as if they were all about to burst out laughing. "What's going on?" she demanded.

"Gotcha!" D.J. cried, breaking into a grin.

Everyone else started laughing. "Boy, you should have seen your face, Steph," Joey said. "You looked like Comet did the day he ate that super-hot chili powder I left on the counter."

Stephanie tried not to smile. "*Very* funny," she muttered. "I knew you guys were joking."

Michelle grinned. "Admit it. We got you good!"

"Don't worry, Steph," Danny said, passing Darcy the pancakes. "You three still have a ride to the mall this morning."

"Don't you mean you four?" Michelle asked. "I want to see to the new mall, too. *Remember*, Dad?"

Stephanie grinned at Michelle. "Well, then pass the maple syrup," she told her sister. "The sooner we finish eating, the sooner we can get to the mall!"

"Do you believe this place?" Darcy asked.

Stephanie gazed around at the escalators, and at the glass elevators in the mall. Each level was outlined in glowing neon. Beneath her feet, the floors were paved with clear plastic blocks that changed color as you stepped on them.

"It's like a cross between a mall and a club," Allie said.

"Or something from the future," Stephanie added. Ahead of them she saw Danny, Joey, and Michelle step through a colorful arch and into a glass elevator. Joey waved as they were whisked to one of the upper levels. They would all meet in a few hours to go home.

Stephanie pointed at the large fountain in the center of the mall. People hurried toward it from all directions. "I wonder what's going on over there?"

"There's one way to find out," Darcy said. She led the way toward the crowd.

When Stephanie, Darcy, and Allie reached the edge of the plaza, Stephanie saw a huge sign posted near the fountain. A crowd of girls surrounded it. " 'Celebrate our grand opening in style,' " she read aloud. " 'Enter the Miarra San Francisco's Most Fabulous Sisters Modeling Contest.' " She turned to her friends. "That sounds like fun. Maybe we should do it."

Allie nodded. "We can all be models together!"

Stephanie and her friends quickly scanned the rest of the sign.

"Wow!" Allie breathed. "The grand prize is a shopping spree in five stores in the mall."

"Only five?" Stephanie asked.

"They're all designer boutiques," Allie explained. "With really incredible clothes. Plus you get a dinner with the Miarras at Pacific Rim—that restaurant at the north end of the mall."

Dinner with the Miarras, Stephanie thought. She pictured herself in the ritzy new restaurant. She and the two glamorous designers would sit around a fancy table, getting to know one another. Then they would comment on Stephanie's natural fashion sense and tell her that she should become a designer—just like they are!

"Bummer!" Darcy said. "You can enter the contest only if you have a sister. See? It says since Fiona and Felicia Miarra are sisters, the contest is for 'San Francisco's most fabulous sisters.' "

"Sisters?" Stephanie echoed. "I wonder if I could get D.J. to enter with me. She's a great dresser, and she's pretty, too."

Stephanie read on, feeling more excited by the second. Each pair of sisters that entered the contest would get free modeling lessons and a professional makeover. They would also get to take part in a real fashion photo shoot. For the final contest they had to provide their own clothes, which were supposed to reflect their special sense of sisterly style. That's what they would be judged on.

"This is perfect," Stephanie said. "D.J. and I have great sisterly style. As soon as I get home, I'm going to ask her to enter the contest."

Allie stood on tiptoe to see the sign. "It looks like there are more rules and stuff written at the bottom," she pointed out.

Stephanie couldn't see the rest of the sign. She made her way through the crowd, trying to get a better look. As she moved through a knot of people, she felt her elbow bump someone.

"Oops! Excuse me," Stephanie apologized. She turned to see whom she'd bumped. A tall, slim girl with shiny dark hair gazed back at Stephanie. Her big green eyes were fringed with long lashes. She wore a lavender minidress.

She was the prettiest girl Stephanie had ever seen. I hope she's not entering the contest, she thought. She'll win for sure.

"It's okay," the girl said with a perfect smile. "My name is Rianne. Are you going to enter the contest?"

"I'm thinking about it," Stephanie said, trying to sound casual. "I have to see if my sister D.J. can do it with me. What about you?"

Rianne nodded. "I'm going to enter with my sister Rhonda." She gestured to a tall girl standing nearby.

Stephanie gulped. Rhonda was Rianne's twin. Rhonda looked exactly like her gorgeous sister, except that her dark hair was cut in a short, stylish bob. "That's great," Stephanie said weakly. "Good luck." Then she walked back to her friends.

"Who was that girl you were talking to?" Darcy asked. "She's really pretty."

"Tell me about it," Stephanie said. "She has a twin sister. And they're both entering the contest. Talk about competition!"

"Don't worry about it." Allie placed a hand on Stephanie's shoulder. "You and D.J. have something special."

"I hope so," Stephanie said. "Anyway, a little competition is a good thing, right? It just means that D.J. and I will have to try our hardest."

"So what did the small print say?" Darcy asked. "What are the other rules?"

"I forgot to look," Stephanie admitted.

"There are some entry forms over there." Allie pointed to a table set up next to the fountain. "I bet the rules are printed on them. Be right back," she said, and walked away.

When Allie returned, she handed a form to Stephanie.

"What does it say?" Darcy asked.

"There's a schedule of the events. A photo shoot class on Monday, a runway modeling class on Wednesday, and a makeover on Friday," Stephanie said. "The fashion show is in one week—Saturday afternoon."

Stephanie read the rules aloud to her friends. " 'All contestants must be U.S. citizens,'" she said. " 'Parents must sign permission slips,' blah, blah, blah . . ." Then her gaze stopped short. "Wait a second," Stephanie said. "All contestants must be age eighteen or under?"

"What?" Allie said. "But that means . . ."

"I know." Stephanie felt her heart sink. "D.J. is too old to enter the contest with me!"

# Chapter
# 2

So how does it feel to be entering the working world at age ten, Michelle?" Danny joked as he and Joey walked her down the wide central aisle of the mall.

Michelle giggled. "It feels great! Thanks again for helping me get this part-time job, Dad. And thanks for helping me keep it a secret from Stephanie."

Danny gave her a quick hug. "Wild horses couldn't drag it out of me. After all, it's for a good cause."

Joey tugged gently on Michelle's strawberry-blond hair. "I'd say earning money for

Stephanie's surprise birthday present is an *excellent* cause."

Michelle smiled. Stephanie's birthday was coming up in two weeks, and Michelle wanted to buy her something really special. There was just one problem. Michelle didn't have any money.

Then her dad found out that their neighbor, Mrs. Cruz, was opening a taco stand in the new mall. He asked if Michelle could help out there for a week, and Mrs. Cruz said yes!

Michelle gazed ahead, trying to see where the food court began. It was a long walk from where they entered the mall. Michelle didn't mind, though. It meant that they were less likely to run into Stephanie and her friends.

Joey slowed down as they passed a bookstore. "I want to see if they have any new joke books," he said. "I'll catch up with you guys later."

Michelle walked a little faster. She didn't want to be late on her very first day.

"Michelle! Mr. Tanner!" a voice called.

Michelle turned and saw her best friend,

13

Cassie Wilkins, running out of a music store. Her other best friend, Mandy Metz, trailed behind her.

"Hi, guys," Michelle said. "I forgot you said you were coming to the mall today."

Danny greeted Michelle's friends, then glanced into the music store. "I'll be right back," he said. "I just want to say hi to Cassie's parents."

"Hurry up, Dad." Michelle pointed to her watch. "Mrs. Cruz is waiting."

Danny smiled. "That's my girl," he said. "You're acting like a responsible employee already!" He winked and walked into the store toward Mr. and Mrs. Wilkins.

Cassie turned to Michelle. "Are you excited about your job?"

"I still can't believe you're working for a whole week in the new mall," Mandy added. "It's *so* grown-up!"

Michelle shrugged. "It's the only way I could make enough money to buy Stephanie that silver bracelet she wants."

"You're lucky your neighbor decided to open a taco stand," Cassie said.

"I know." Michelle nodded. "It's called El Taco Loco. 'The crazy taco.' "

Danny came out of the store with Cassie's parents. "Ready to go, Michelle?" he asked.

"I'm ready." Michelle crossed her fingers. "Wish me luck," she told her friends.

"Good luck," Mandy said.

*"Buena suerte,"* Cassie added. "That means 'good luck' in Spanish. I saw it on TV."

"Thanks." Michelle giggled. "I mean, *muchas gracias!"*

She and her father left the others in front of the music store and continued down the aisle. Just before they reached the taco stand, Danny stopped.

"Now, remember," he said. "Mrs. Cruz is doing you a favor by giving you this job. You need to show her you're a hard worker."

"I will," Michelle promised. Then they hurried to the taco stand. Mrs. Cruz, a plump woman with short black hair and a friendly smile, stood behind the counter.

"Hello, Mrs. Cruz," Danny said, shaking the woman's hand. "I'm here to deliver your new part-time worker."

"Wonderful." Mrs. Cruz beamed at Michelle and held out her hand. "Welcome to El Taco Loco, Michelle."

Michelle shook her new boss's hand. "Thanks for giving me this job," she said. "I really appreciate it."

"You're quite welcome," Mrs. Cruz replied, smiling again. "Now, let's go in the back and get you started right away, okay?"

The woman's expression was so sunny that Michelle couldn't help grinning back. "Okay, Mrs. Cruz."

"I'll be back to pick you up at the end of your shift," Danny told Michelle. "Good luck!"

Michelle and Mrs. Cruz said good-bye to Danny. Then Mrs. Cruz gestured for Michelle to come behind the counter. "Let me show you around," the woman said.

Two cash registers rested on the long front counter. At one of them, a young woman in an apron was making change for a man who was buying a soda.

"What do I do first," Michelle asked eagerly. "Learn how to use the cash register? Take some orders?" She could already picture herself ringing up sales, punching a button to make the change drawer pop out, and handing out food to happy customers.

"Oh, no, no, dear," Mrs. Cruz said with a chuckle. "You won't have to spend much time up here in the front at all. The full-time employees and I will take care of working the cash register and taking orders."

Michelle nodded but felt a tiny bit disappointed. Still, she was sure there were lots of interesting things to do in the back, behind the scenes.

She followed Mrs. Cruz through a narrow doorway. The kitchen was laid out in a square, with shiny steel counters along three sides. The other wall held a big refrigerator and a closet.

Michelle looked around curiously. A man with dark hair and a bushy mustache was stirring a bubbling pot of melted cheese on a large stove. "I'm Charlie," he said to Michelle.

"Hi, Charlie!" Michelle replied. "I'm Michelle."

"And I'm John," a short blond man chopping lettuce on a wooden chopping block said. "Welcome to El Taco Loco!"

"Thanks!" Michelle smiled. She couldn't wait to get started. She saw herself standing at the counter, dicing onions into perfect little cubes with John and Charlie. This was going to be fun!

Mrs. Cruz turned to Michelle. "Are you ready to start your first job?" she asked.

"You bet," Michelle declared, pushing up the sleeves of her sweatshirt. "What do you want me to do? Help Charlie melt the cheese? Chop some lettuce and onions?"

Mrs. Cruz chuckled. "No, no, dear," she said, patting Michelle on the shoulder. "That's not the sort of thing you'll be doing. John and Charlie will take care of the cooking."

"Oh." Michelle felt another twinge of disappointment. If I'm not going to cook and I'm not going to take orders or use the cash register, then what *am* I going to do? she wondered. But Michelle didn't want to seem ungrateful. She smiled at Mrs. Cruz. "Okay," she told her. "Just tell me what to do, and I'll do it!"

"That's the spirit," Mrs. Cruz said. "First, let

me give you your very own El Taco Loco apron just like the rest of the crew."

She bustled over to the wall near the refrigerator, where a row of white aprons hung. Mrs. Cruz held one out to Michelle. It had a picture of a taco with little arms and legs waving wildly. EL TACO LOCO was printed above it.

"Cool." Michelle took the apron and tied it around her waist. It made her feel as if she were wearing a uniform, just like a real employee. "How do I look?" she asked.

"Wonderful!" Mrs. Cruz leaned over and pulled something out of a small box on the counter. "Now, one more thing before we get you started," she said cheerily. "Let's put your hairnet on."

"My what?" Michelle stared at the item in Mrs. Cruz's hand. It looked like a tangled clump of string.

Mrs. Cruz stretched it out, and Michelle saw that it was a net shaped like a cap. "You need to wear this when you're working near food," she explained. She helped Michelle slip it on over her hair.

The hairnet felt weird. Michelle didn't even want to think about what she looked like wearing it. Oh, well, she thought. It's not as if any of my friends are going to see me in the kitchen.

Michelle turned to Mrs. Cruz. "Okay," she said, tucking the ends of her hair under the hairnet. "Now what?"

Mrs. Cruz reached under the counter and dragged out a large cardboard box. "This new shipment of paper cups came in yesterday," she explained. "All the sizes are mixed up together. I'd like you to sort them by size—small, medium, and large. Then count them to make sure they're all there."

That's it? Michelle asked herself. She glanced at the big box of paper cups. But counting cups is so boring!

"When you're finished, I'll show you where to put them away." Mrs. Cruz smiled. "Good luck, dear. I'll come back in a few minutes to see how you're doing."

"Okay. Thanks again for giving me this job, Mrs. Cruz," Michelle said. She had to give the job her best try—even if it wasn't very exciting. "I won't let you down."

"I'm sure you won't." Mrs. Cruz patted Michelle on her hairnet, then headed out to the front of the taco stand.

Michelle pulled out a handful of paper cups from the box and sighed. Wearing a hairnet and counting cups wasn't exactly the most glamorous job in the world. But that didn't matter. I'm going to be the best employee El Taco Loco has ever seen, she decided. And I'm going to buy Stephanie the birthday present she really wants!

*STEPHANIE*

# Chapter
# 3

I can't believe it," Stephanie moaned. "D.J. missed the cutoff age by one year. And I really wanted to be in that fashion show. Now I don't even have a *chance* to hang out with Fiona and Felicia Miarra! Of all the rotten luck. I mean I—"

"Uh, Steph," Allie interrupted. "D.J. isn't your *only* sister, you know."

"Yeah," Darcy added. "What about Michelle?"

Stephanie gasped. "I didn't even think of Michelle for the modeling contest. I mean, she fits all the requirements. She's under eighteen, and she *is* my sister . . . and I bet she'd love to do it, too!"

She looked at the other girls clustered around the sign. Most of them were much older than Michelle. But who cares? Stephanie thought. Michelle and I will make awesome models. Besides, it would be fun to do something like this together.

"So is Michelle in?" Allie asked.

"Michelle's in," Stephanie replied.

"What are you guys going to wear?" Darcy asked.

"Good question." Stephanie glanced around at the stores surrounding them. "Luckily, we're in the perfect place to find the answer. Let's shop!"

Before long, she and her friends were flipping through racks of shimmery shirts and dresses.

"I can't believe you're going to be a model, Steph," Allie said. "In a real fashion show, in front of real, professional fashion designers. Aren't you nervous?"

"No way," Stephanie said, trying to sound serious. "I was born to model. I'll probably be discovered at the contest and whisked away to Paris for a fabulous new life as a supermodel." She tried to hold a straight face, but burst out laughing instead.

"Well, I hope you get discovered," Darcy said with a giggle. "Then you can take us along as you jet all over the world." She reached out and flipped Stephanie's long blond hair to the side. "Yes, you will definitely need your own personal fashion consultant."

"Two," Allie chimed in. She flipped Stephanie's hair to the other side.

"Okay, you're both hired!" Stephanie grinned. "So, fashion consultants"—she pulled a pale pink top off the rack and held it up to her face—"do you think this color works for me?"

"Totally," Allie told her.

Then Darcy switched into reporter mode. "Stephanie Tanner, the look for spring!" She pretended to hold a microphone out to Stephanie. "Miss Tanner, how does it feel to have the whole world staring at you?"

Stephanie pushed away Darcy's hand. "No, no," she said in a haughty voice. "No last names for me. Just call me Stephanie. You know, like Naomi or Cindy or Madonna."

Allie laughed. "Good one, Steph," she said. "Hey, wait. Madonna's not a supermodel."

Darcy grinned. "But she's famous. *Almost* as famous as Supermodel Stephanie."

Stephanie smiled and took one last glance at the sale rack, then she turned and headed for the exit. "Come on, there's nothing that's really great here. Let's keep shopping. If I want to wow the judges next week, I have to make sure Michelle and I are *oozing* style."

They stepped out into the mall. "Hey, look." Allie pointed to a store just ahead. "I didn't know there was a Zoom store in this mall. I love their clothes."

"Me, too," Stephanie said eagerly. She bought a lot of her clothes at the Zoom in downtown San Francisco. They had the hottest fashions.

The three friends hurried into the store. Stephanie gazed around at the tables stacked with multicolored T-shirts and sweaters. "This could be the place," she said. "I'm sure I'll find something great to wear here."

Darcy nodded. "Zoom definitely has the Stephanie Tanner—I mean just *Stephanie*—sense of style."

Stephanie laughed. Then she let her eyes roam around the store. "Let's see. Do I want to go totally California casual? Or more dressy and elegant?"

"What do you think of this?" Darcy held up a green cotton T-shirt dress with purple trim around the collar and sleeves. "Pretty cute, huh? And it's on sale."

"Hmm." Stephanie looked over the dress. "That would go perfectly with these." She pointed to her clunky purple sneakers.

Allie nodded, her eyes sparkling. "Try it on!"

"Okay," Stephanie agreed. She took the dress from Darcy and went to the fitting room. Moments later, Stephanie came out with the dress on. She spun around to show off the outfit.

Darcy clapped her hands. "It's awesome!"

"Definitely perfect for you," Allie agreed. "It's just what you need for the contest."

Stephanie gazed in a mirror. She twisted

back and forth, watching the short skirt flare up around her legs. "I guess we're going for the sporty look," she said, taking one last look in the mirror. "I love it! Now I need one just like it for Michelle."

Darcy flipped through the kids' racks. She held up a purple T-shirt dress with green trim. "This isn't exactly the same style, but it's close."

Stephanie examined the label. "It's Michelle's size," she said. Then she glanced down at the price tags on the dresses. She felt her hopes sink. Even though the prices were slashed, the two dresses were more than she could afford. "Forget it," she said. "I can't get them. I don't have enough money."

"What?" Darcy gasped. "But you *have* to get them. They're perfect!" She dug into her pocket and pulled out a handful of crumpled bills and a few coins. "Here, I have, um, nine dollars and twenty-seven cents. You can borrow that."

Allie checked her own pockets. "I've got a ten," she said, offering the money to Stephanie.

Stephanie smiled at her friends. They were always there for her. "Thanks, guys," she said, taking the money. "I really owe you one."

"Actually, you owe us nineteen dollars and twenty-seven cents," Allie pointed out with a grin.

Stephanie checked her own wallet and grinned back. "I think I have just enough now." She changed back into her own clothes and paid for the two dresses. Then she and her friends left the store.

"I guess we should go home," Allie said. "No cash, no flash."

"Just because we're out of money doesn't mean we can't check out the rest of the mall," Stephanie pointed out.

Darcy nodded. "Let's go."

Stephanie, Allie, and Darcy wandered down a wide aisle, looking into each store they passed. A large group of girls crossed to the other side of the concourse, each one holding a shopping bag from Zoom.

Stephanie shifted her own bag from one hand to the other as a horrible thought popped into her head. "I hope no one else decides to wear the same dress in the contest next Saturday," she said to her friends. "I mean, lots of people shop at Zoom. What if these dresses aren't original enough?"

"Don't worry," Allie assured her. "No one else will look as good in them as you and Michelle."

"I hope that's what the judges think," Stephanie replied.

The girls paused to admire a dress in the window of an expensive-looking boutique called Verve. As they did, Stephanie saw a familiar face inside the shop.

"Hey, look," she said. "That girl Rianne is in there."

Allie peered in. "Her sister, too," she said. "See? She just came out of the dressing room. She's the one wearing that sparkly silver dress."

"Whoa!" Stephanie murmured. "It's gorgeous! It looks like it's made out of tiny silver mirrors."

"It is awesome," Darcy agreed. "And fits like it was made for her."

Stephanie sighed. "I hope she's not buying

that dress for the modeling contest." She watched as Rhonda twirled around in her dress. Meanwhile, Rianne pulled another dress from a rack and disappeared into the fitting room. The dress was the same style as Rhonda's, but instead of silver, it was bronze.

A moment later both sisters emerged wearing their own clothes. They walked to the cash register, carrying the dresses.

"Suddenly a T-shirt dress doesn't seem all that special," Stephanie said glumly.

"Let's go in and see if you find anything you like," Darcy suggested. "If you do, you can return the Zoom dresses and use the money to buy something here instead."

As Stephanie and her friends entered the shop, Rianne and Rhonda turned away from the sales counter and spotted them. "Hi," Rianne called with a smile. "Stephanie, right? Remember me—Rianne?"

"Um, sure," Stephanie said, returning the smile. How could I forget? she thought. "Hi, Rianne. These are my friends, Darcy and Allie."

Rianne smiled at Darcy and Allie. "This is my sister, Rhonda."

## And the Winner Is . . .

"Hi," Rhonda said. "We just bought our dresses for the modeling contest. Are you guys going to be in it, too?"

Allie shook her head. "No, just Stephanie," she said. "She's entering with her sister Michelle."

Rianne caught sight of the shopping bag in Stephanie's hand. "You bought something at Zoom? Rhonda and I love that store!" she exclaimed. "Their clothes are so cute. What did you get?"

Stephanie hesitated. She really didn't want to show Rianne and Rhonda the dresses, especially since she was thinking about returning them. "Oh, nothing important," she said. "I'm still looking for a special outfit for the contest."

"Well, good luck." Rhonda smiled. "We'll see you on Monday at the photo shoot!"

"Bye," Stephanie said. She waited until the sisters were gone, then turned to Allie and Darcy. "Okay, come on. You've got to help me find something here that's just as cool as their dresses."

Darcy was already looking around the

31

store. She picked out a yellow rayon dress with a camisole top and a flared skirt. "What about this?" she said.

Stephanie's eyes widened. "It's fabulous!" she said. She picked up the hanger and held the dress against herself, glancing at her reflection in a mirrored wall. "I totally love it! This will be perfect for the contest."

"Maybe you should try it on," Allie suggested.

"Okay," Stephanie agreed. "I'll just go and—" She fell silent as she caught a glimpse of the price tag. "Uh-oh," she said. "Maybe not. This isn't exactly in my price range."

Darcy looked over Stephanie's shoulder at the tag. "You're definitely right about that."

Stephanie gave the dress a last look. "Too bad," she said, and put it back on the rack. "Let's keep searching."

Fifteen minutes later, Stephanie sighed. "I think I've looked at every piece of clothing in this store," she said. "But everything is way too expensive."

Allie nodded. "Yeah, you'll need a supermodel's salary before you can buy anything here."

"Come on," Stephanie said. "We'll have to try some cheaper stores. But first we can stop back in Zoom to return these." She shook the shopping bag with the T-shirt dresses in it.

Darcy gave her a doubtful look. "Are you sure you don't want to keep them, just in case you don't find anything you like better?" she asked.

Stephanie shook her head firmly. "No way. Michelle and I will look pretty pathetic next to what Rhonda and Rianne are wearing. I have to find something just as good. I don't want to mess up my big chance to meet the Miarras."

"Okay," Darcy said. "Just remember, even after you return those dresses, you still won't have a whole lot of money to spend."

"You may be right," Stephanie admitted. "But I refuse to give up. This just means I have to come up with something that's totally unique!"

# Chapter
# 4

See you on Monday, Mrs. Cruz," Michelle said. She untied her apron and smiled at her boss. She almost forgot about her hairnet, but then she felt the elastic on her forehead and pulled that off, too. She tucked it in the pocket of her apron.

Mrs. Cruz came over and patted her on the shoulder. "Good job today. You're the best new worker I've had in a long time."

"Thanks." Michelle waved and hurried out from behind the counter.

She whistled as she left the taco stand, thinking about Mrs. Cruz's words. It was nice to know that she was doing a good job, even if the actual work wasn't what she thought it would be.

So what if the job is a little boring, Michelle thought as she looked around for her father. After just five more days, I'll have enough money to buy Stephanie that bracelet. I can't wait to see the look on her face when I give it to her!

She spotted Danny coming toward her. "Hi!" he called. "Sorry I'm a little late, Michelle. How was your first day on the job?"

"Great, Dad," Michelle said. "Just great!"

Michelle and her dad walked toward the bench near the mall entrance, where the whole family was supposed to meet to go home. Glancing ahead, Michelle saw that Stephanie, Allie, Darcy, Joey, Becky, and the twins were already there.

"Go ahead and join them, Michelle," Danny said. He paused in front of a housewares store. "I just want to stop in here and check the price of their rubber gloves. Don't want to get dishpan hands!"

Michelle nodded and hurried toward the

others. Stephanie was sitting on the bench, talking to her friends. But as soon as she saw Michelle, she rose to her feet. "Hey, Michelle!" she cried, rushing toward her. Darcy and Allie were close behind. "You'll never guess what we're doing next weekend."

"What?" Michelle asked.

Stephanie grinned. "We're going to be models!"

"Huh?" Michelle asked, confused. "What are you talking about?"

"There's a modeling contest next Saturday," Stephanie replied. "You know, like a fashion show? But it's only for sisters. Sisters like us!"

Michelle grinned. "You want *me* to be in the contest with you?" she asked. "We're going to be models together?"

"Uh-huh!" Stephanie nodded. "I just signed us up."

"Wow!" Michelle started to feel as excited as Stephanie looked. She was so glad that Stephanie wanted to do something cool with her. Since they were four years apart in age, they didn't really get to hang out a lot together. Stephanie was always with her friends. It would definitely be fun to do something like this, just the two of them. "That will be so cool!" Michelle added.

"I know," Stephanie said. "We get to go to a photo shoot class on Monday after school."

"Then there's the modeling class on Wednesday afternoon," Darcy put in.

Allie nodded. "And don't forget about the makeover on Friday."

"Of course, the first thing we have to do is figure out what to wear," Stephanie said. "The judges want to see our sisterly style."

"I can't wait!" Michelle cried.

"But we have only a week to come up with something awesome, so it's going to take some fast work."

Work? Michelle almost groaned out loud. She totally forgot about her job at the taco stand. How am I going to have time for photo shoots and modeling classes when I'm supposed to be at El Taco Loco every afternoon? she wondered.

Michelle couldn't tell Stephanie about her job. She wanted Stephanie's present to be a surprise. That's why Michelle was working in the first place. There's no way she could keep the job *and* be in the modeling contest.

"Um, Steph?" Michelle began. "Are you sure you really want to do this? The contest, I mean."

Stephanie gave her a surprised look. "What do you mean? Of course I'm sure. Aren't you?" she asked. "You just said you couldn't wait."

"Well . . ." Michelle hesitated. "I'm not totally sure, I guess. It kind of sounds like a lot of work. You know, with all those classes and everything . . ."

Darcy giggled. "Yeah, but we're not talking about advanced algebra here."

"Right," Stephanie said. "We're talking modeling. Makeovers. *Fun* stuff."

Michelle shrugged. She didn't want to look at her sister's disappointed face. "Why don't you ask D.J. to do it with you instead?" she asked, staring at her sneakers.

"I can't. D.J. is too old," Stephanie explained. "Michelle, this fashion show is really important to me. Besides, don't you think it would be fun for *us* to enter together? It'll probably be the coolest thing we've ever done as sisters!"

Michelle couldn't argue with that, and she didn't want to miss out on spending time with Stephanie, either. She had to figure out a way to do both things. She just had to!

STEPHANIE

# Chapter
# 5

"This contest is going to be the greatest," Stephanie told Michelle that night at dinner. "I'm so glad we're doing it together. And I have the perfect idea for our outfits. It's totally cool and totally unique. Something that will give us extra-special style!"

Michelle wiped her mouth with a napkin. "What is it, Steph?"

"Well, first I bought us dresses at Zoom," Stephanie told her, "but then I returned them."

"But Zoom is the coolest store in the mall," Michelle cried. "How come you returned the dresses?"

## And the Winner Is . . .

"Because a lot of kids shop in Zoom," Stephanie said, "and I want us to wear something totally original. Something the judges will really notice. That's why we're going to *make* our dresses!" she cried. "Dad said that there might be some of Mom's old dress patterns in the storage room."

"That's right," Danny replied. "Mom used to sew all the time. I bet there's even some fabric down there."

"And I think I saw her sewing machine somewhere, too," D.J. added.

"I got an A in the fashion design class I took last term in school," Stephanie said. "My teacher thought I had natural talent. Now is my chance to prove it."

"Well . . ." Joey rose from the table. "You definitely have your work *cut* out for you," he said, laughing. "Get it? *Cut* out?" He made a scissors motion with two fingers.

Everyone at the table groaned.

"So did you start reading that new joke book yet?" Jesse asked.

Becky nudged him in the arm.

"They can't all be winners." Joey laughed

**4 1**

again. "I guess I'll have to *design* some new jokes. Get it, Steph? *Design* a joke?"

Stephanie shook her head as Joey took his plate into the kitchen. "Joey needs all the help he can get," she said, still shaking her head. "And so do I. Darcy and Allie are coming over after dinner to help with the dresses."

"Can I help, too?" Michelle asked. "Making dresses would be fun."

Stephanie shook her head. "I'm not sure about that," she replied. "These dresses have to be perfect."

"But you're making one for me, too, right? I should be able to help." Michelle sat up in her seat. "Just tell me what to do, Steph. I won't get in your way. I promise."

"I guess it couldn't hurt," Stephanie told Michelle.

Then the doorbell rang.

"That's probably Darcy and Allie now." Stephanie jumped out of her seat. "May I be excused?" she asked her father.

"Me, too?" Michelle stood up.

Danny nodded. "Just remember to clean up in the storage room when you're through. I don't want it messier than it has to be in there, okay?"

"We promise," Stephanie said before she answered the front door. She knew that her dad always liked every room in the house to look as perfect as possible—even a room filled with junk.

Stephanie led Michelle, Darcy, and Allie downstairs to the storage room, which was right next to Joey's apartment. She flipped on the light and looked around the small, cluttered area. "Let the search begin!"

Darcy walked over to a large metal trunk and lifted the lid. "This trunk is filled with old clothes," she reported.

"Go ahead and check it out," Stephanie said. "I'm going to look by the window. I think that's where my mom's things are." She crossed to a stack of cardboard boxes on the far side of the room. Then she reached for the one on top—and hesitated.

This is Mom's stuff, she thought sadly. I didn't even know that she liked to sew until Dad told me today.

"What's wrong?" Allie asked.

43

"I just feel a little weird about going through my mom's things," Stephanie admitted.

Allie came to stand beside Stephanie. "I bet she'd feel really good about it. Kind of like she's still part of your life, helping you."

Stephanie gave her friend a quick hug. "Thanks," she said. "That's a really nice way to think about it."

She opened the top box. It was filled with chipped dishes. Stephanie closed it and moved on to the next one, which was stuffed with musty old books.

Darcy laughed out loud. "These are classic!" she cried, and held up a pair of little kid's shorts. They said STEPHANIE in big orange letters across the seat.

Michelle shut her eyes tight. "This has got to be a bad dream. Tell me I'm not seeing those shorts again, Steph!"

"Michelle and D.J. had ones with their names, too," Stephanie explained. "Dad got them when we went to Disneyland years ago. He thought if we wore them, he wouldn't lose us."

"Did it work?" Darcy asked.

## And the Winner Is . . .

Stephanie grinned. "No. The shorts were so embarrassing, none of us would wear them. So instead he got us hokey straw hats. Michelle gave hers to Donald Duck and got lost, anyway."

Allie pulled a large piece of flowered cloth from a plastic bin. "Could you make something out of this, Steph?" she asked.

Stephanie inspected the material. "I don't think it's big enough for two dresses," she replied, and opened another box. This one was filled with pots and pans.

Now Stephanie was beginning to worry. She *had* to find something she could use for the contest. She wanted to have dinner with Fiona and Felicia Miarra more than anything. How cool would it be to tell them that she made two fabulous dresses out of old stuff from the storage room? Who knows? Maybe she could even open her own design company someday.

Stephanie opened another carton and sighed when she found a moth-eaten blanket. She removed the blanket and gasped at what was underneath.

"Did you find something good?" Michelle asked, hurrying over.

"I sure did," Stephanie replied. "It's Mom's old sewing machine. She ran her hand along the smooth blue metal of the machine. She felt more hopeful already.

A few minutes later Allie let out a cry. "I just found a whole box of sewing stuff! There's no fabric," Allie said. "But lots of thread and buttons and boxes of straight pins. And some old dress patterns."

Darcy hurried over and picked up the patterns. "Hey, some of these are pretty funky," she commented. "They must be from the seventies."

Stephanie nodded, looking over Darcy's shoulder. "Stop!" she cried as Darcy flipped to a short, swingy long-sleeved dress pattern. "What about that one? It's cool, and it looks simple."

Allie grabbed the pattern and examined the directions that came with it. "You're right," she said. "It doesn't even have a zipper—just one button. We can definitely handle this!"

"What do you think, Michelle?" Stephanie

asked. She showed the pattern to her little sister.

Michelle checked out the picture. "I love it!" she declared.

"Great! Then all we need is fabric and we're set!" Stephanie placed the pattern on the floor and continued her search.

Michelle looked up from a box in the corner. "Hey, I think I found something," she called. She pulled out a bundle of heavy fabric from the box.

Stephanie smiled when she saw the bright blue and green psychedelic pattern.

"Whoa," Allie gasped. "Intense colors!"

"It's so cool!" Darcy added.

"I remember that," Stephanie said, feeling a stab of excitement. She hurried over and took the fabric from Michelle. She held it up for a better look. "It's the leftover material from those curtains that used to be in Dad's room when you were a baby, Michelle."

"I think our search is over," Darcy said. "Those colors are perfect for a funky seventies dress."

"You're right," Stephanie agreed. "This is it.

We've found our outfits!" She was feeling more psyched by the second.

"What are we waiting for?" Michelle asked.

Stephanie and Darcy grabbed the fabric. Allie carried the sewing box, and Michelle took the pattern. Then they all headed upstairs to get to work.

Stephanie and Darcy laid out the material on the living room area rug. "Tape measure," Stephanie requested, holding out her hand.

Allie pulled it out of the sewing box and slapped the tape measure into Stephanie's hand. "Tape measure," she repeated.

Stephanie took Michelle's measurements, then she asked Allie to take hers.

"Pattern," Stephanie said, pointing to the floor.

Darcy grabbed the funky pattern and laid it over the fabric. "Pattern is ready, doctor," she said, smiling.

"Straight pins," Stephanie requested, looking at Michelle.

Michelle handed her a small box and giggled. "Straight pins," she replied.

Stephanie carefully pinned the pattern to

the material. "All set," she said when she'd finished. "Who wants to cut?"

"I'll do it," Michelle said eagerly.

"I don't think so," Stephanie replied.

"Let me try," Darcy offered. She picked up the scissors and tried to trim the fabric, but the blades wouldn't cut through.

"Press harder," Stephanie urged her.

Darcy gripped the scissors and grimaced. "I'm pressing as hard as I can, but the scissors just aren't working."

Stephanie frowned. "They've got to. Let me try." She took the scissors and leaned over the pattern. A few seconds later, she gave Darcy an apologetic look. "You're right," she said. "This fabric is too thick for scissors." She lifted her long hair off her neck. "Okay, time for Plan B. What else can we use to cut it?"

"A blowtorch?" Darcy said with a weak smile.

Just then Joey walked into the living room. "Hey, girls," he greeted them. "What are you up to?"

Stephanie quickly explained their problem.

"What about the utility knife in the toolbox?" Joey suggested. "It'll cut through just about anything."

"We'll try it!" Stephanie said. She jumped to her feet and started to rush out of the room.

Joey grabbed her by the elbow. "Hold it, Steph," he told her. "Like I said, the utility knife is pretty sharp. You'd better check with your dad first about using it."

"I'll go ask him." Michelle offered. She hurried out of the room. A few minutes later she returned. "Dad says it's okay for Stephanie to use the utility knife as long as she wears his leather work gloves while she's cutting. And as long as we all promise to be very, very careful."

"No problem," Stephanie said. "I'll be right back." She raced to the storage room and returned with the utility knife and Danny's heavy leather gloves.

She slipped on the gloves. Slowly, she pressed the button on the knife that edged the blade out of its plastic case.

"That thing looks sharp. Be careful," Allie reminded her.

"I will." Stephanie bent over the blue and

green fabric again. She had to use a fair amount of pressure, but the knife cut through the fabric. "Yes!" she murmured. "Now we're getting somewhere."

Carefully, she followed the pattern. She sliced along the bottom of the dress, up each side, and around the sleeves. She brushed some sweat from her forehead with the back of her hand. Cutting such thick, heavy fabric wasn't easy.

"There," she said at last. She ran the knife around the bottom hem. "Done!"

"Just *your* dress," Darcy pointed out. "You still need to cut out Michelle's."

Stephanie sat back on her heels. "We can do that in a minute," she said. "First let's make sure this came out right."

She grabbed the piece she had cut, held it against her body, and glanced down. It looked pretty good. In fact, the fabric seemed even cooler now that it had a shape.

"Wow!" Michelle said. "I can't wait to see mine!"

"Uh, Steph?" Allie asked from her spot on the floor. She seemed worried. "I think we have a problem here."

"What?" Stephanie replied. "Don't tell me we don't have enough fabric for both dresses. I'll scream."

"That's not it." Darcy sounded nervous. "But I think someone else might be screaming soon. Namely, your dad."

"Why?" Michelle asked. "What's the matter?"

With a gulp, Allie reached down and pulled up a funky dress-shaped piece of the living room rug.

"Oh, no!" Stephanie gasped in horror. "I ruined the rug when I cut out the dress. Dad's going to ground me for life!"

# MICHELLE

## Chapter 6

"Ready to go, Michelle?" D.J. asked Monday after school. D.J. had offered to drive Michelle, Stephanie, Darcy, and Allie to the mall.

Michelle jumped up from the couch and pulled on her jacket. She was glad that Stephanie and her friends were still upstairs.

"Listen, D.J.," Michelle whispered. "I need to ask you a favor. A big one."

"What?" D.J. sounded distracted. "Where's Stephanie? We need to leave if you want to be on time for that photo shoot."

Michelle took a deep breath. "That's sort of what the favor is about." Talking fast, she explained about her secret job. So far, her father and Joey were the only ones in the family who knew about it.

"Wow," D.J. said. "You have a job? Way to go, Michelle. That's so mature."

"Thanks," Michelle said. "But now I need to figure out a way to escape from Stephanie long enough to run over to El Taco Loco and explain why I'm going to be a little late. I tried to call Mrs. Cruz, but the phone has been busy forever."

D.J. looked doubtful. "Are you sure Mrs. Cruz won't mind?"

Michelle shrugged. "You know how nice she is," she said. "I think it will be okay. But after the photo shoot I have to work at the taco stand. I need you to help me so Stephanie doesn't suspect anything."

"What do you mean?" D.J. asked.

Michelle explained her plan. "After the photo shoot, you could say you need me to go shopping with you. Then I can go work at the taco stand instead of staying with Stephanie and her friends. It'll be easy."

"Well, I guess I could do that." D.J. still

looked a little doubtful. "What's our story going to be when you have to sneak away to talk to Mrs. Cruz?"

Michelle shook her head. "I don't know," she admitted. "I'll have to come up with something on the way to the mall."

D.J. flicked on her turn signal. "Almost there," she announced.

Michelle felt her stomach flip over. It was almost time for action. The problem was she still didn't know how she was going to get away from Stephanie and explain things to Mrs. Cruz.

Maybe I'll just say I need to use the bathroom, she thought.

D.J. pulled into a parking space near the mall's main entrance. "Last stop, everybody out," she called.

"Thanks for the ride, D.J.," Stephanie said. "See you later." She hopped out of the car and started toward the front doors. Darcy and Allie were right behind her.

Michelle waited, hopping from one foot to the other as D.J. locked the car. "Don't forget,

Stephanie can't know what we're up to," she whispered.

"I know, I know." D.J. dropped the keys into her backpack. "Don't worry. Your secret's safe with me."

"Come on, Michelle!" Stephanie called from the sidewalk in front of the entrance. "We're supposed to meet at the fountain in ten minutes."

"Uh . . ." Michelle didn't know what to say.

"You three go ahead," D.J. called back before Michelle could think of something. "It looks as if Michelle's shoelace just broke. I'll help her fix it, then bring her over to meet you. Okay?"

Stephanie didn't look very happy about that, but she shrugged. "Okay," she called. "I'll tell them you're on your way, Michelle. But try to hurry."

Michelle gave D.J. a grateful look. "We will!" she answered.

D.J. and Michelle waited as Stephanie and her friends entered the mall. A minute later, D.J. and Michelle walked through the doors.

D.J. gazed around the mall. "I think the

coast is clear," she said. "Do you want me to walk over to the food court with you?"

"You don't have to," Michelle answered. "I just need to stop there long enough to explain things to Mrs. Cruz. Then I'll run over to the photo shoot. It's simple."

D.J. nodded. "I guess it's okay if you go by yourself." She smiled. "After all, you're old enough to have a job now, right? Just make sure you go straight to El Taco Loco and then right from there to the fountain plaza. Okay?"

"I will," Michelle said. "Thanks again, D.J. I'll see you after the photo shoot. Don't forget, you have to tell Stephanie I'm shopping with you later, okay?"

"Got it. I'll see you then." D.J. waved, then turned to enter a nearby store.

Michelle took off down the aisle at top speed. She knew she had to hurry if she wanted to make it to the fountain plaza in time for the start of the photo shoot. There wasn't much time, but at least everything was going as planned.

Michelle was breathless when she arrived at

El Taco Loco. She saw Mrs. Cruz standing behind the counter.

"You're eager to get to work today," Mrs. Cruz said cheerfully. "That's what I like to see!"

"No," Michelle gasped. "Uh—I mean, I am eager. But first I need to go do something really important for a little while. It will probably take only a few minutes."

Mrs. Cruz put her hands on her hips. "Now, Michelle. You know you have a job to do here."

"B-b-but it's important," Michelle stuttered.

"Your dad told me how *important* this job was for you. That's why I gave it to you." Mrs. Cruz smiled and came out from behind the counter.

"But—" Michelle tried again.

Mrs. Cruz shook her head, still smiling. "You'll be able to take your break in two hours. Surely whatever you have to do can wait until then, right?" She put her arm around Michelle and led her into the kitchen. "Now, come, let's get your hairnet and apron on. I want you to put stamps on some envelopes and then help Charlie unpack the new shipment of burrito shells. There's always lots to do around here! No time to waste!"

Michelle meekly wrapped her El Taco Loco apron around her waist and slipped on her hairnet. Now she would never get to the photo shoot in time. Stephanie was going to be so angry.

A sick feeling formed in the pit of her stomach. This isn't the way my plan was supposed to work, she thought miserably. This isn't the way it's supposed to work at all!

# Chapter
# 7

Stephanie, Allie, and Darcy hurried toward the fountain in the mall. Stephanie's mind was already on the photo shoot. She thought about all the different poses she and Michelle could do in front of the camera.

"Are you *sure* your dad didn't notice the rug?" Allie asked.

"Dad doesn't suspect a thing," Stephanie replied. "Actually, he told me he really likes the new furniture arrangement." She shook her head. "I still can't believe I messed up the rug!"

"Don't worry so much," Darcy told Allie.

"That Super Glue is supposed to hold anything together. Even rugs."

"I know," Allie said. "But all we did was glue the piece of rug back in place, then rearrange the furniture on top of it. Can that really work?"

"I hope so," Stephanie said. "Because if it doesn't, I'll be grounded until I'm forty." She hoped the glue would work until she figured out a way to tell her dad about the rug without making him go ballistic. But she couldn't think about that right then. "Can you guys come over tonight and help work on the dresses? I haven't even started sewing yet!"

Darcy shook her head. "I can't. I have that book report due for English tomorrow, remember?"

"And I have an extra piano lesson tonight," Allie added. "For my recital next month. Sorry."

"That's okay. Michelle and I can probably get a lot done ourselves." Stephanie smiled, remembering how excited her sister was when she found the cool fabric. "You know, it's nice to be doing something like this with

Michelle. I don't really spend enough time with my little sister."

A large crowd of girls was already gathered at the fountain plaza. Stephanie's pulse started to race. She was so excited.

"Look at those guys pushing around those huge lights," Darcy said. She glanced up at the skylights high above them. "I guess it's not bright enough in here for the pictures."

"Check it out." Stephanie saw a tall, auburn-haired woman wearing a red embroidered vest standing next to the fountain. She had a fancy-looking camera around her neck and was talking to an older woman with salt-and-pepper hair.

"That red-haired woman must be the photographer," Allie said. "I like her vest."

Just then the older woman stepped away from the photographer and walked up some steps and onto a small stage near the fountain. She cleared her throat and spoke into the microphone. "Attention, fashion show contestants," she said. "My name is Ms. Nolan, and I'm one of the judges for the San Francisco's

Most Fabulous Sisters Fashion Show. Is everybody ready to have some fun today?"

The crowd cheered.

Ms. Nolan smiled and held up her hands for quiet. "That's what I like to hear! Remember, we will be looking for enthusiasm on Saturday as well as a great sense of sisterly style. The photo shoot class will begin shortly. Please remember that you must attend all three classes to be able to participate in the fashion show." She clapped her hands. "Okay, contestants, please make your way to the area behind me and wait there with your partners."

Stephanie scanned the plaza for her sister. "Hey, speaking of partners, do you guys see Michelle? She should be here by now."

Darcy glanced around. "I don't see her," she said. "But it's hard to tell with all these people here."

"We'd better find her," Stephanie said. "I'll walk around the fountain this way, and you guys go the other way. By the time we meet back here, one of us should have found her."

The three friends set off. Stephanie circled

the fountain in a wide arc, looking carefully at everyone she passed. But Michelle was nowhere around. Maybe Darcy and Allie found her, she thought.

When she spotted her friends coming toward her, Michelle wasn't with them.

"No luck," Allie called out.

Stephanie tried to stay calm. "You didn't find her, either?"

Darcy pointed to where the photographer's assistant was setting up a large tripod. Most of the contestants already stood in the area behind Ms. Nolan. "Looks like they're almost ready to start," she said.

Stephanie checked her watch. "Come on, Michelle," she said under her breath.

Ms. Nolan came bustling toward them, a clipboard in her hand. "Ready, girls?" she asked cheerfully.

"Not exactly," Stephanie admitted. "My sister isn't here yet."

"I see," Ms. Nolan replied. "Well, I'm sure she'll be here soon. In the meantime, why don't you join the others? The photographer wants to give you a few pointers before you get started." She smiled at Stephanie and moved on.

Stephanie turned to her friends. "I'm starting to get worried. Michelle's not usually late, and neither is D.J." She bit her lip. "Will you guys do me a favor and go look for them again?"

"Will do," Darcy said.

Allie nodded. "We'll be back as soon as we can."

Stephanie shot them a grateful look, then hurried toward the other contestants.

"Welcome," the photographer began. She was very pretty, with high cheekbones and huge, dark eyes. "My name is Lorna. Today I'll be taking pictures of each pair of sisters," she said. "I'll ask you to get up onstage and move around, smile, put your arms around each other, do whatever feels fun and natural. You'll be using the raised area around the fountain as your stage both for these photos and also for the actual fashion show on Saturday."

Stephanie glanced over toward the fountain. She couldn't stop worrying about her sisters.

Rianne raised her hand. "Should we smile or look serious in the pictures?" she asked.

"Good question," Lorna said. "I hope you'll do a lot of smiling, since this is supposed to be fun. If you and your sister are having a good time, you'll end up looking happy in the pictures."

Stephanie nodded. She and Michelle would definitely have fun in front of the camera—if Michelle ever got there.

"Okay, let's get started," Lorna said.

Get started? Stephanie thought. But—they can't. Michelle still isn't here! Where could she be? she wondered, feeling more anxious than ever. What happens if Michelle doesn't make it in time?

Lorna picked up her camera and smiled at the group. "Who would like to go first?"

A pair of girls stepped forward and walked up onto the stage. Stephanie wasn't sure whether to watch them or keep a lookout for Michelle. She tried to do both at the same time.

Most of the contestants seemed a little nervous when they first climbed onstage. They giggled and moved stiffly. But Lorna talked to them all calmly and cheerfully as she snapped pictures, which helped the girls relax.

Soon Rianne and Rhonda were on the stage. Unlike the others, they seemed relaxed right from the start. Stephanie was impressed with the way they moved from pose to pose. First they stood close together, looking at the camera, then they linked arms and looked at each other, then they stood back-to-back.

"Wonderful," Lorna exclaimed, snapping photo after photo. "Terrific, girls! One more—perfect!"

Wow, Stephanie thought. Rianne and Rhonda are really good. They look like professional models already! If we want to beat them on Saturday, Michelle and I—

Michelle. Suddenly, out of the corner of her eye, Stephanie caught a glimpse of a young girl with strawberry-blond hair running across the plaza. She felt a flood of relief. At last!

Then the blond girl turned toward her and Stephanie saw that it wasn't her little sister after all. Where *is* she? Stephanie wondered.

Soon the second-to-last pair of sisters finished their set, and Stephanie's stomach turned in knots. She and Michelle were supposed to be next.

Lorna scanned the group. "Is that everyone?" she asked. Then she spotted Stephanie. "You with the pretty blond hair. You haven't taken a turn yet, have you?"

"Not yet." Stephanie stepped forward with a gulp.

"Where's your partner?" Lorna asked.

At that moment, Stephanie saw Allie and Darcy rushing toward the fountain. Stephanie's heart sank. Michelle wasn't with them.

Stephanie swallowed hard. Maybe the judges would let her go on by herself for now. Hopefully, Michelle would show up soon.

"Um . . . she's a little late," Stephanie finally answered. "Why don't I just go ahead? She won't mind."

Lorna looked surprised. She glanced over at Ms. Nolan, who stood nearby. "Will that be all right?"

Ms. Nolan frowned. "I'll allow it this time. But this is a contest for *sisters*. If this happens again, I'll have to disqualify you."

Stephanie let out the breath she was holding. No matter how worried she was about her sisters, she was glad she didn't get kicked out of the contest. "Thanks," she told Ms. Nolan and Lorna. "Michelle will be here for the next class, I promise."

Stephanie gave Lorna her name, then hurried up the steps onto the stage. It felt strange to be up there alone after watching all the others pose in pairs. But she tried to remember all the things Lorna said about relaxing, moving around, and acting natural.

"Nice," Lorna said, her camera clicking away. "Very good. Now hold that pose for a second."

Stephanie paused, gazing straight into the camera. Then she changed to a different pose, glancing off to the side. I'm the only one without a partner, Stephanie thought. This would be much more fun if Michelle were here.

Stephanie finished her turn without any problems—except that she was the only girl there without her sister. She joined the other contestants at the side of the stage.

"Thanks for your good work today," Lorna

told everyone. "I'll see you again on Saturday, when I take pictures at the fashion show. In the meantime, have fun at the other classes this week!"

"Thank you," Stephanie chorused with the others. But she wasn't really thinking about the contest anymore.

As Lorna turned to talk to Ms. Nolan, Stephanie rushed over to Darcy and Allie. "You didn't find D.J. and Michelle?" she asked anxiously.

Allie shook her head. "We searched everywhere. We even checked to make sure the car was still in the parking lot."

"So where *are* they?" Stephanie ran her hands through her hair and glanced around again. "I don't even know where to look next." Just then she spotted D.J. hurrying toward them.

"Hi!" D.J. said breathlessly. "Sorry I'm late."

Stephanie grabbed her sister's arm. "Thank goodness you're okay!" she said. "Where's Michelle? She missed the photo shoot class. We almost got disqualified."

"Michelle?" D.J. repeated blankly. She looked around. "Isn't she here with you?"

Stephanie's heart began to pound. Michelle was only ten years old. If she wasn't with her, and she wasn't with D.J. . . .

D.J. slapped her forehead with her hand. "Wait a minute!" she said. "I almost forgot. I told Michelle to wait for me at the shoe repair store. I had to run back to the car because I forgot my backpack. On the way there I got lost—you know, new mall—so I thought I'd stop by and let you know we were okay. So it's all my fault she didn't make it to the photo shoot. I'm really sorry."

"Oh." Stephanie frowned. It wasn't like D.J. to be so scatterbrained. Still, her story explained why Michelle never showed up. "It's okay, I guess. As long as everyone's fine."

D.J. nodded. "I'd better go get Michelle."

"I'll come, too," Stephanie said. "Where's this shoe store?"

"That's okay," D.J. said quickly. "I'm sure you three have shopping to do. I can get her myself. I'll check the directory." She laughed again. "I guess I should have done that in the first place. Duh!"

Stephanie gave her older sister a puzzled

look. "All right," she told her reluctantly. "We'll meet you by the entrance in an hour, okay?"

"Great," D.J. said, and hurried off.

Allie watched her with a frown. "That was weird."

"I know." Stephanie shrugged. "But at least Michelle's okay."

"Besides," Darcy added. "I don't think the classes count as much as the actual fashion show."

"And Michelle and I are going to model something really different." Stephanie's stomach fluttered when she thought about being on the runway in front of the Miarras. "Fiona and Felicia are going to be so impressed with our outfits," she said excitedly. "All I have to do is sew them up, and everything will be totally perfect!"

As soon she got home, Stephanie brought the swirly blue and green fabric and her mother's sewing machine into the laundry room. Thanks to the rug disaster, she was behind schedule and couldn't afford to lose any more time. Even worse, Michelle had to study for a math test and couldn't help her.

She set up the old sewing machine on the craft table and plugged it in. Stephanie quickly pinned the two halves of the dress together the way her sewing teacher had taught her.

It wasn't easy to get the heavy layers of fabric into the little space between the needle foot and the base of the machine. "Why do they have to make it so narrow, anyway?" she muttered.

Finally, the fabric was in place. Stephanie pushed the lever to lower the needle. It rested on top of the blue and green material, but Stephanie couldn't get it to go through.

That's okay, Stephanie thought. The fabric is a little thick, but when I start the machine, everything will be fine.

The sewing machine buzzed loudly as she pressed on the foot pedal. Then the needle pushed into the fabric, but it didn't come out.

Stephanie pushed the pedal all the way to the floor. The sewing machine whirred louder, but the needle still didn't move. "It's stuck!" she cried, quickly releasing the pedal.

Stephanie didn't know what to do next. She had to start sewing the dresses that night or else she might not have them ready for the fashion show.

In a panic, Stephanie yanked the blue and green fabric from the sewing machine. *Snap!*

"Oh, no!" she gasped as the needle broke squarely in two!

Stephanie rested her head in her hands and closed her eyes. She could just see Rianne and Rhonda at the fashion show, prancing down the catwalk in their awesome outfits from Verve.

Then she opened her eyes and watched her blue and green fabric slip onto the floor in a heap.

What am I going to do now? she wondered.

# MICHELLE

## Chapter 8

"Thanks for driving me to the mall, Uncle Joey." Michelle gave her uncle a big hug. "I owe you one." It was Wednesday afternoon. Joey and Michelle were standing in the center plaza of the new mall.

"No problemo." Joey said. "I had to go back to the bookstore, anyway. That last joke book I bought was a lemon. I need to get another one. Can you make it to the taco stand on your own from here?"

Michelle nodded. She knew how to get to the food court by now. "Thanks again!" Michelle waved as Joey turned toward the bookstore. Then she hurried on her way.

Michelle had asked Joey to pick her up after school and bring her to the mall early. She figured if she started work earlier, she could take her break earlier. Michelle would take the modeling class with Stephanie, then rush right back to work. Nobody would suspect a thing.

"You're early, Michelle," Mrs. Cruz said when she reached El Taco Loco. "But I've got plenty for you to do."

Michelle quickly tied on her apron and shoved her hairnet over her strawberry-blond hair. "I'm ready!" she cried.

"Good. Why don't you go ahead and sort those bills we talked about yesterday? Then you can start rolling up the extra pennies."

Michelle sat at a little desk built into the counter by the closet and got busy. The more work she finished, the happier Mrs. Cruz would be about letting her take her break early.

With a sigh, she picked up the top sheet of a huge stack of papers. Michelle was supposed to put each invoice into the correct file. She stuck the first bill into a folder marked LET-

TUCE. Then she picked up the next one and started searching for the NAPKINS file.

I have only two more days at the taco stand, Michelle thought as she looked for the folder. At the end of the day on Friday, Mrs. Cruz will pay me, and then I'll buy Stephanie her birthday present. Even better, I can go to the fashion show on Saturday without having to sneak out of work!

After Michelle finished sorting invoices, she picked up the jar of extra pennies. She stacked the change in roll after roll of paper tubes.

Charlie walked by just as Michelle added the last penny to the last roll. "Wow, Michelle," he said. "You're a real speed demon today."

John looked over the counter and grinned. "You'd better watch out, Charlie," he joked. "If Michelle gets any better, she'll take your job."

Michelle smiled. "Not a chance," she told John. "Friday is my last day, remember?"

Then Michelle glanced at her watch. Only fifteen minutes until the modeling class, she realized. I'd better head over to the fountain so I'm not late.

Untying her apron, she hurried to the front of the taco stand. Mrs. Cruz stood at the counter, handing a customer a tray of enchiladas. "Finished with the pennies already?" Mrs. Cruz asked Michelle.

"Yup," Michelle said. "I was wondering if I could take my break now."

"Well, I suppose that would be all right," Mrs. Cruz agreed. "But first, could you do me one favor?"

"Sure. What is it?" Michelle asked, hoping it would be a *quick* favor.

"I need to call the bakery that makes our tortillas," Mrs. Cruz said. "Could you get me their card from the address file on the desk? The name is Rico's Tortillas."

"No problem." Michelle heaved a sigh of relief as she sped back to the desk. It would take only a few seconds to find the right card for Mrs. Cruz. Then she could meet Stephanie for the modeling class.

Michelle flipped through the long plastic box that contained cards with all of Mrs.

Cruz's business contacts written on them. She quickly found the address and telephone number for Rico's Tortillas.

"Got it." Michelle yanked the card out of the file—too hard. The plastic file box bounced off the edge of the desk and landed on the floor with a crash. File cards scattered across the entire floor.

"Oh, no!" Michelle's hands flew to her face, dropping the Rico's Tortillas card somewhere in the mess.

"Whoa, Michelle," Charlie said with a laugh. "What a wipeout!"

"We'll have to start calling you Miss Butterfingers!" John laughed, too.

Michelle gazed at the floor in horror. Almost every single card had come out of the box! She had to clean this up fast!

"Do you have the number for Rico's Tortillas yet, Michelle?" Mrs. Cruz asked, coming into the kitchen. She gasped when she saw her card file emptied on the kitchen floor.

"Uh . . . not *exactly*." Michelle stared at the big jumble of cards on the floor and gulped. "But I'll find it as fast as I can!"

*STEPHANIE*

# Chapter
# 9

"Allie, thanks again for helping me fix my mom's sewing machine," Stephanie said over the phone. "I felt terrible about breaking it." It was Wednesday after school.

"No big deal," Allie replied. "I just replaced the needle. We have a sewing machine at home. It happens to my mom all the time." She paused. "But I wouldn't use the sewing machine on that fabric again. It's too thick."

"No way," Stephanie assured her. "I don't want to risk breaking it again." She flexed her fingers. "It's hand sewing from now on. In fact, I'm going to work on the dresses for the fashion show before Michelle and I go to our modeling class today."

"Great," Allie said. "Darcy and I will meet you at the mall after my piano lesson. We want to cheer you guys on, okay?"

"Okay," Stephanie replied. "See you there!" she added, and hung up the phone.

Danny walked into the living room. "I *thought* that was you talking on the phone. Do you want a snack?"

Stephanie shook her head and headed for the stairs. "No time, Dad," she said. "I'll be working on our dresses till we have to leave for the mall."

"Oh," her father replied. "Michelle already went over to the mall with Joey. I told them we'd meet them there."

"Cool." Stephanie ran up the stairs, taking them two at a time. She grabbed the blue and green fabric and sewing box from her desk, then raced back down to the living room. The light was better there, and there was more room to work.

Stephanie settled down cross-legged on the floor. She laid out the fabric pieces in front of her. She sewed the top seam on her dress the day before, but it took so long to pull the needle through the heavy fabric for each stitch.

"This is going to take forever," Stephanie muttered as she threaded a needle. She grabbed the scissors from the sewing box and snipped the thread. She dropped the scissors on the floor and sighed. "I'll never finish this on time."

D.J. walked in just in time to overhear her. "Talking to yourself again, Steph?" she teased.

Stephanie looked up with a sigh. "I don't know what to do," she told her older sister. "I have only three days to finish these dresses, but it's taking forever to sew the seams."

"Are these the famous dresses you've been talking about?" D.J. asked. She glanced at the picture on the pattern envelope, which was lying on top of the sewing box. "Cool pattern," she said. Then she picked up one of the dress pieces. "Wow, I can see why you're having trouble. This stuff is pretty heavy. You probably need a special industrial sewing machine or something."

"Got any ideas about where I could find

one?" Stephanie asked, only half joking.

D.J. looked thoughtful. "No, but I think I know what you could try instead," she said. "Sometimes when I need to fix a hem but don't have time to sew it, I use Super Glue to hold it up."

Stephanie's eyes widened. "That's it!" she cried. "After all, the Super Glue worked great on the—" She gulped, stopping herself just in time from mentioning the rug. "Um, I mean it's supposed to work on any kind of fabric. So I'm sure it will work on our dresses, too. Thanks for the idea!"

"Anytime." D.J. smiled. "I think I have some Super Glue in my desk if you want to borrow it."

"That's okay. There's a whole tube in the toolbox downstairs," Stephanie said. "I can use that."

"Good luck," D.J. replied, and headed for the stairs. "I wish I could stick around and help, but I have a paper due tomorrow."

"Don't worry about it," Stephanie said. "You've helped me plenty already."

Stephanie raced to the storage room and

found the tube of glue she used for the rug. Then she returned to the living room and laid out her fabric pieces again. "Hmm," she muttered to herself. "I just have to figure out where to glue each seam. And I can't make any mistakes!" Stephanie knew that once the Super Glue took hold, it would be impossible to pull the pieces apart.

Finally, when she was satisfied that everything was ready, she uncapped the glue and leaned over the fabric. "Here goes," she said, giving the tube a little squeeze. The glue shot straight out and landed on the scissors and the floor.

"Yikes!" Stephanie grabbed the scissors and dropped them on the pattern envelope before they could stick to the floor. Then she leaped up and raced into the kitchen.

"Hi, Steph," Danny said. He looked up from cleaning the vegetable crisper. "How's the sewing going?"

"Fine," Stephanie said breathlessly. She grabbed a handful of paper towels. "Just great. See ya!"

She ran back to the living room, praying the

Super Glue didn't dry super-fast. She dropped to her knees and quickly mopped the puddle of glue off the floor. She noticed a few drops splattered on some of the fabric and dabbed them off.

Stephanie sat back and wiped her brow. Close one, she thought. Then she glanced at the scissors on top of the pattern envelope.

"Oops. Almost forgot about those." Stephanie reached out and grabbed for the scissors, but they were already starting to stick to the paper.

Uh-oh, Stephanie thought. Her dad would not be thrilled to find an envelope stuck to his scissors. Carefully, she peeled the scissors away. I'd better wipe off the blades, she decided. But when Stephanie tried to open the scissors, she couldn't. They were glued shut!

Quickly, Stephanie picked up the tube of glue. She stared at the directions on the side. There's got to be something here about how to *unstick* this stuff, she thought.

" 'Use on wood, plastic, fabric . . .' " she read. " 'Bonds permanently. The glue that never lets go!' "

"Oh, terrific," Stephanie muttered. Feeling guilty, she shoved the scissors under the couch. I'll buy Dad a new pair as soon as I get my allowance, she told herself.

Stephanie returned her attention to the dresses. Once she calmed down and concentrated on what she was doing, the glue worked like a charm. All she had to do was squirt it along the seams, exactly where she would have sewn, and press the pieces together for a few seconds.

"And presto!" She held up the body of her dress and gazed at it. This looks so good, she thought. I *should* go into fashion design.

She picked up the right sleeve to attach it and kept working from there. Soon her dress was ready and Michelle's was almost finished. The only problem was that Stephanie couldn't seem to find the left sleeve she'd cut out for the smaller dress.

Her father came out of the kitchen. "Ready to go, Steph?" he asked.

"In a second, Dad," she answered. "Where is that stupid thing?" she muttered to herself as her father went to the closet to get his jacket. She pawed through the extra fabric. No sleeve. She turned in a slow circle, scanning the room. No sleeve. She got down on her hands and knees and checked under all the furniture. She spotted the scissors under the couch, but there was still no sign of the missing sleeve for Michelle's dress.

"Let's go, Steph," Danny called from the door.

"Coming." Stephanie glanced around the room once more. She let out a sigh of frustration. Where did it go? She grabbed her coat and followed her dad out the door. I'll have to find it as soon as I get home, she thought.

Allie and Darcy were waiting for Stephanie when she reached the fountain a little while later. Most of the contestants were there already, milling around and waiting for things to get started.

Stephanie looked over at the stage. Ms. Nolan was standing there, making notes on her clipboard.

"Is Michelle here yet?" Stephanie asked her friends.

Darcy winced. "Not yet."

Stephanie felt a horribly familiar stab of worry. "But Joey brought her to the mall ages ago. She was supposed to meet me here."

"Don't worry," Allie said. "You've got time. It's not like the class has started yet."

Ms. Nolan walked up to the microphone. "Welcome back, contestants!" she began. "Now we'll begin our runway class."

Stephanie gulped and exchanged a glance with her friends. She couldn't believe this was happening—*again*. Where was Michelle?

Ms. Nolan introduced the day's instructor—a former model named Yvette. Yvette was *really* tall. Her straight black hair hung down her back almost to her waist.

"Hello, ladies," Yvette said with a brilliant smile. "Are you all excited about becoming models on Saturday?"

Most of the contestants whooped and cheered. Stephanie clapped. *You'd better show up this time, Michelle!* she thought.

Yvette smiled and held up her hands for quiet. "Some people think being a model is easy," she said. "But there's a lot to know if you want to be a good model. Today we'll concentrate on how to stand and walk to show off the clothes to their best advantage." She walked to the center of the stage. "Let's start with the classic runway walk," Yvette said. She looked into the distance and strode across the stage in a practiced, graceful walk. Her hips swayed. Her glossy hair swung as she turned.

But Stephanie barely noticed. She was still watching for Michelle. Where was she this time?

"Let me give you a couple of hints," Yvette went on. "First, don't walk too fast when you're onstage. You want to give people enough time to see you. Second, try to relax and have a good time. If you do that, you'll naturally look better and move more smoothly." She smiled. "Got all that? Okay, I'm going to call your names one at a time. Please come forward and walk across the stage so we can see you move."

The first contestant Yvette called on was a cute red-haired girl with freckles. She walked back and forth across the stage several times while Yvette called out suggestions.

Stephanie glanced at the stage a few times, but mostly she kept watching for Michelle. She was worried about her, but she was also kind of annoyed. Michelle knew how much this contest meant to Stephanie, and she knew when the class started. How could she forget? Especially after Monday's disaster!

"All right," Yvette said a few minutes later when the red-haired girl's sister finished. She glanced at the notebook in her hand. "Next, could I see either Michelle or Stephanie Tanner on the stage, please?"

"That's me!" Stephanie called out. "I'm Stephanie Tanner."

Yvette smiled at her. "Okay, Stephanie," she said. "Let's see you walk."

Stephanie nodded and smiled. But her stomach was churning. Soon everyone would know that her sister wasn't there—again. What would Ms. Nolan say this time? Would she kick her out of the contest?

She decided not to think about that until she had to. She slipped off her coat, and she handed it to Allie. "Wish me luck," she murmured.

Allie's eyes widened. "Steph, wait!" she whispered.

"I *can't*," Stephanie whispered back. "It's my turn!" She hurried through the crowd and up the stairs.

Stephanie straightened her spine and gazed into the distance. Then she started across the stage. She tried to picture the models she'd seen on TV. She tried to make her steps long and fluid and slow.

Make it look as if you've been doing this all you life, she told herself as she put one foot in front of the other. Make it look easy. Make it look cool. Make it look—

She paused. Was she imagining things, or was that laughter she heard? She sneaked a quick peek at the audience that was gathered to watch the lesson. Several people in the front of the crowd were snickering. Yvette, who was standing right next to the stage, looked startled and confused.

What's going on? Stephanie wondered. It can't be because I don't have a partner. Yvette hasn't even asked about Michelle.

She took a few more steps, did a dramatic

spin—and stopped. Darcy was jumping up and down and waving at her frantically.

Maybe she's trying to tell me that Michelle finally showed up, Stephanie thought hopefully.

Stephanie took a closer look at her friends. Allie's cheeks were pink and her eyes were wide. Darcy pointed one finger at her rear end. Then she jabbed the finger toward Stephanie.

Huh? Stephanie thought. She reached behind her and gasped. Something was flapping off the back of her pants. Twisting around frantically, she caught a glimpse of a swirly blue and green fabric. It looked like—could it be? a sleeve. Hanging off her jeans like a *tail?*

Mortified, Stephanie yanked at the blue fabric. It wouldn't come loose, though her jeans pulled out so far, she was afraid they might rip if she pulled any harder. "Oh, no!" she whispered under her breath. "Super Glue!" She felt her face turn redder than ever as even more people started laughing.

This has got to be the most embarrassing thing that has ever happened to anyone in the history of the world, Stephanie thought as she hurried toward the steps. She grabbed her coat from Allie and quickly pulled it back on, hiding the sleeve from view.

"Okay, settle down, everyone," Yvette called. She glanced at Stephanie. "That was, um, very good, Stephanie. Now let's see Michelle Tanner onstage, please."

This is doubly embarrassing, Stephanie thought miserably. She'd just made a fool of herself on the runway, *and* her sister hadn't showed up. Ms. Nolan's words from the photo shoot ran through her mind. *If it happens again, I'm afraid we'll have to disqualify you.*

"Michelle Tanner," Yvette called out. "Are you here?"

Stephanie swallowed hard.

Allie rested her hand on Stephanie's shoulder. "What are you going to do, Steph?" she whispered.

Feeling desperate, Stephanie grabbed Allie's arm. "Allie," she whispered. "Go up there! You've got to pretend you're Michelle!"

# MICHELLE

## Chapter
## 10

Excuse me!" Michelle cried over and over. She dodged people left and right, rushing to the fountain plaza. "Sorry!"

She had finally found the number for Rico's Tortillas and cleaned up the rest of the address cards for Mrs. Cruz. Now Michelle was on her half-hour break, but she was late for the modeling class. *Really* late! Stephanie is probably very angry with me, Michelle thought. She just hoped the class wasn't over yet.

Michelle arrived at the fountain plaza just in time to see Stephanie shove Allie toward the stage. For a second, Michelle couldn't figure out what was going on.

How can Allie enter the contest? she wondered. She doesn't have any sisters.

"Good to see you, Michelle," a tall woman in front of the stage said to Allie.

Then Michelle figured it out. Allie is pretending to be me! Hey, that's not fair. She's not Stephanie's sister. *I* am!

"No! Wait!" Michelle cried. She raced toward the stage. "Wait, I'm Michelle Tanner! I'm here!" She pushed her way to the stage.

"Michelle!" Allie sounded relieved. She turned and hurried down the steps. "I was just— um, I mean—well, just go ahead."

"What's going on here, girls?" the tall woman asked. She looked at Michelle. "If you're Michelle Tanner, who is this?" She pointed at Allie.

"Uh, nobody." Allie smiled weakly and joined Stephanie and Darcy in the audience.

Michelle flashed a bright smile. "So what am I supposed to do?" she asked the woman.

"Walk across the stage as if you were a

model," the woman said. She looked very confused.

Michelle strode across the stage. Carefully, she turned, paused, and walked back. "How was that?" she asked.

"Not bad," the woman said. She asked Michelle to do it again, instructing her to walk more slowly and to hold her chin up higher. "Much better. All right, who's next? I'd like to see either Rianne or Rhonda Le Brec?"

Michelle wasn't listening to the instructor anymore. She marched up to Stephanie with her hands on her hips. "Okay, what's the big idea?" she demanded. "Why was Allie pretending to be me?"

"What are you so mad about?" Stephanie replied. She crossed her arms over her chest. "You're the one who didn't show up when you were supposed to."

"I showed up," Michelle protested. "I'm here, aren't I?"

"Yeah, *now.*" Stephanie shrugged. "But you were so late that I was afraid we were going to get disqualified!"

"Come on, guys," Allie broke in. "It doesn't

matter now. All that matters is that you're both here."

"I don't get it, Michelle," Stephanie continued. "I signed us up for this contest because it sounded like fun. I thought you were excited about it, too. So why are you trying to ruin it for both of us?"

Before Michelle could answer, the instructor frowned at them. "Girls!" she said. "We're trying to hold a class here."

"Sorry, Yvette," Stephanie said.

Michelle wished she could tell Stephanie the real reason she was late, but she couldn't. And she was still a little annoyed at Stephanie.

What kind of rotten big sister ditches her sister just for being a little late? she thought grumpily. Especially when she's late only because she's working to get her sister a nice birthday present.

Finally, the class ended. Michelle didn't remember much that Yvette told them about walking like a model. But she paid more attention when the instructor mentioned the next event.

"Don't forget, girls," Yvette said. "You'll be getting your makeovers on Friday, same time, same place. Don't be late!"

"Did you hear that, Michelle?" Stephanie glared at her. "She said *don't be late*."

Michelle clenched her fists. "I've got to go," she said. "I'm supposed to, uh, meet Joey at the sneaker store to help him pick out some new basketball shoes. See you." She spun and hurried away before Stephanie or her friends could say a word.

When Michelle returned to El Taco Loco, Mrs. Cruz was waiting with a new list of chores. For once, Michelle was glad. The harder she had to work, the less time she had to think about what had happened.

But later, as she refilled the napkin dispensers, Michelle began to think that being angry with Stephanie wasn't exactly fair. This contest is important to Stephanie, she thought. She didn't want to get kicked out. That's why she got Allie to step in. And Stephanie had no way of knowing that I was late because I was working to get money for her birthday present.

## And the Winner Is . . .

Michelle pushed some more napkins into the metal napkin holder and came to a decision. She wasn't going to let Stephanie down again. She wasn't going to miss any more of the modeling contest. Not one more minute. Not one more second.

I just have to figure out a way to work it out, she thought.

"It's almost quitting time," Mrs. Cruz told Michelle a little while later. "And I have a little surprise for you!"

Michelle smiled wide. "What's the surprise, Mrs. Cruz?"

"Achoo!" Charlie came up front from the kitchen, blowing his nose. "Mrs. Cruz, I'b really sick. I'b going to have to stay hobe toborrow, okay?" he asked with a stuffy nose.

"Oh, yes," Mrs. Cruz replied. "Please get some rest."

Charlie nodded. He blew his nose again and headed out.

"Get well soon, Charlie!" Michelle called. She watched as he slowly walked into the mall.

"I'm glad Charlie told me he wasn't feeling

well," Mrs. Cruz said. "I don't want anybody to come into work when they're sick."

Michelle's eyes widened. She just got a great idea. On Friday, she will tell Mrs. Cruz that she was sick. Mrs. Cruz won't want her to come into work, and Michelle will be able to get a makeover with Stephanie. It's perfect!

"Well, back to my surprise for you, Michelle." Mrs. Cruz pulled an envelope out of her pocket and handed it to Michelle. "I thought I'd pay you a little early."

"Really?" Michelle stared at the envelope. "You mean you're paying me for the week now?" she asked. She peeked into the envelope and saw green bills inside. "This is great!"

Mrs. Cruz smiled. "You're such a responsible girl, Michelle, I know you won't let down your end of our bargain even if you've already been paid," she said. "If you want, you could even take some extra time on your break tomorrow or Friday to shop for you sister's birthday present."

"Thanks, Mrs. Cruz." Michelle glanced down at the money in her hand. She felt a sudden stab of guilt. How could she plan to call in sick when Mrs. Cruz was being so nice to her? But then she remembered how much the modeling contest meant to her sister, and she knew that she had no choice.

I have to call in sick on Friday, she thought. I have to do it for Stephanie.

*STEPHANIE*

# Chapter
# 11

Our outfits are so awesome!" Stephanie exclaimed. It was Friday morning, and Stephanie had finished the dresses for the fashion show—and with twenty-eight hours, twenty minutes, and seven seconds to spare! She was so excited, she could barely sit still for breakfast.

She dug her fork into her father's special tuna omelet surprise. "It was so totally lucky we found those amazing patterns. Not to mention that fabric. We'll be the coolest ones there, right, Michelle?"

Before Michelle could respond, Joey slipped

into his best *Life-styles of the Rich and Famous* voice. "Tomorrow, Miss Stephanie Tanner and Miss Michelle Tanner will be living a life most of us can only dream of—the life of world-famous supermodels. Swimming pools, movie stars . . ."

The whole family laughed. "Hey, Steph?" D.J. asked. "When you're rich and famous, will you buy me a car? I have my eye on a red Corvette."

Stephanie grinned. "Sure," she said. "But being a supermodel could get old pretty fast. Maybe when I get sick of it, I'll just become a famous international fashion designer instead. You know, like the Miarra sisters. I can't wait until they see our outfits."

"Sounds good, Steph." Danny reached for a piece of toast. "Just don't forget to wash those dresses before you wear them, okay? The fabric has been sitting in the storage room for a long time."

Stephanie grinned. "Okay, Dad." Her father was such a clean freak—she was surprised he didn't wash soap before he used it! Still, he did have a point.

"I'll throw the dresses in the washing machine before school," Stephanie told Danny. "That way they'll be fresh and clean for tomorrow's fashion show." Then Stephanie turned to Michelle. "Want to try on the dresses before we wash them?" she asked. "We haven't checked them out with all the accessories."

"Um, okay," Michelle said. "But we have to hurry. I don't want to be late for school."

Once in their room, Stephanie pulled the dresses out of her closet. She held up the smaller one. The new arm she made for Michelle's dress came out pretty good, she thought. She tossed it to Michelle. Then she peeled off her jeans and T-shirt and pulled on her dress. "Ta-da!" she sang, spinning around.

Michelle fastened her button. "It looks nice," she said quietly.

"*Nice?*" Stephanie exclaimed. "Is that all?" She dug through a pile of shoes on her closet floor until she found her sandals with the criss-cross straps.

Stephanie slipped on the shoes. Next she went to the jewelry box on her dresser. She found some blue bangle bracelets and a matching clip for her hair. "I have only one blue hair clip," she told her sister. "One of us will have to wear a white one. Which do you want?"

Michelle just shrugged. "I don't care. You can have the blue one if you want." She flopped on her bed.

"Thanks, Michelle. Are you sure?" Stephanie gave her sister a careful look. She seemed sort of quiet and withdrawn. "Hey, are you okay? You look weird. You're not coming down with a cold, are you?"

Michelle quickly shook her head. "Not yet, I mean, no, I'm not sick."

"Oh, okay." Stephanie put on half the bangle bracelets and gave the rest to Michelle. Then she went to the mirror and carefully fastened her blond hair back in a smooth ponytail. She smiled at her reflection. "Hey, what do you think?"

Michelle blinked. "Wow. You look great!"

"So do you." Stephanie grinned at her. "Are we San Francisco's most stylish sisters, or what?" Michelle didn't answer, and Stephanie's grin faded a little. "Hey, what is it? You sure you're not getting sick?"

"No." Michelle said. "Nothing like that. I guess I'm just a little tired."

Stephanie glanced at her watch. "Oops," she said. "I guess it is getting kind of late. We should be getting to school."

"Okay." Michelle started taking off her dress. "What about washing the dresses?"

"Yikes! I almost forgot." Stephanie slipped her dress over her head, then put on her clothes. "I'll go throw them in the washing machine right now."

She grabbed both dresses and hurried downstairs. Comet followed her. Opening the washing machine, she stuffed both dresses inside and stared at them.

Hmm, she thought. No washing instructions on these Stephanie Tanner originals.

She shrugged and grabbed the laundry detergent, dumping a generous amount into the machine. Turning the knob on the machine to HOT, she hit the button and started the washing cycle.

"There," she said with satisfaction. She bent down to pat Comet. "That should get them clean enough. Even for Dad!"

# MICHELLE

# Chapter
# 12

"Are you ready?" Cassie asked Michelle after school on Friday.

Mandy picked up the receiver on the school pay phone and handed it to Michelle.

"I'm a little nervous," Michelle admitted, taking the phone. "But I'm glad you two are here. I'm not sure I could make this call on my own."

Michelle was really going to do it. She was going to call Mrs. Cruz, pretending to be sick.

"Just hold your nose while you talk," Mandy suggested. "That way it'll sound like you're all stuffed up."

"Good idea." Michelle held her nose with one hand and picked up the receiver with the other. She let go of her nose long enough to take the quarter that Cassie handed her. She dropped it in the slot and dialed the number for El Taco Loco.

When Mrs. Cruz answered, Michelle coughed into the phone and held her nose again. "Hi," she said. "This is Bichelle."

"Michelle?" Mrs. Cruz sounded concerned. "Are you all right, dear? You sound odd."

Michelle sniffled loudly. "I don think I can combe to work this abternoon."

"Oh, dear." Mrs. Cruz sounded worried. "It's too bad you're ill. Especially since today was your last day on the job. But I suppose it can't be helped. Why don't you come in on Monday afternoon and make up the time? Would that be all right?"

"Sure!" Michelle started to sigh with relief, then remembered that she was supposed to sound sick and miserable. She coughed again. "That would be great. I'b sure I'll be better by Bonday."

She felt guilty about getting out of work,

but she just couldn't risk missing today's makeover. Michelle knew how much the modeling contest meant to Stephanie. She didn't want to let down her big sister again.

"All right, then, I'll see you on Monday," Mrs. Cruz said. "Get well soon, dear!"

Once again, Michelle asked Joey to drop her off at the mall right after school. The makeover didn't start for an hour, but now that she had her hard-earned money, Michelle couldn't wait to buy Stephanie's gift.

She was afraid she wouldn't be able to find the exact bracelet Stephanie wanted at the new mall. But she spotted it in the first jewelry store she checked.

"Could I look at that, please?" she asked politely.

"Sure." The clerk opened the case. "It's kind of expensive, though."

Michelle smiled as the man handed her the pretty silver bracelet. "That's okay," she said. "It's a birthday present for my sister."

"Well, she's lucky to have a nice sister like you to buy it for her," the clerk said.

"You're telling me!" Michelle joked.

After making her purchase, Michelle headed to the fountain plaza. This time she was one of the first contestants to arrive. She peeked inside the red velvet box that held Stephanie's bracelet. Michelle couldn't wait for Stephanie's birthday to come. It was a whole week away! Maybe I'll give her the bracelet after the fashion show tomorrow, she thought.

Michelle glanced around for Stephanie and slipped the box inside her jacket pocket. She watched a few makeup artists set several large suitcases on folding tables. When they snapped them open, Michelle saw that they were filled with eye shadow, blush, and lip gloss in every color of the rainbow.

This will be cool, she thought. I am going to wear makeup—just like Stephanie and D.J.

"You're here already!" Stephanie cried when she arrived a few minutes later. "Let's go stand near the fountain," she suggested. "Maybe we'll get to go first."

"Okay." Michelle followed her sister over to the center of the action. She gasped when a pair of very tall, *very* pretty dark-haired twins approached them. Michelle thought they looked like professional models.

"Isn't this cool?" asked the girl with longer hair. "I can't believe we're getting real make-overs."

"I know." Stephanie introduced Michelle to the two sisters, Rianne and Rhonda. "It's going to be awesome. Right, Michelle?"

"Definitely." Michelle had been so busy trying to fit in the week's events with her job, she'd barely thought about the fact that she was going to be in a real fashion show. It really was pretty exciting now that she thought about it.

"Michelle, smile," Stephanie told her. "Here comes Ms. Nolan—the big cheese."

"Hello, girls," Ms. Nolan said. "We're just about ready to get started. Would one of you like to volunteer to go first?"

"You can go first if you want, Michelle," Stephanie offered.

"Thanks," Michelle said, smiling at her sister.

Ms. Nolan led Michelle to a tall chair on the

stage. "A makeup artist will be here in a moment." Then she walked away.

A moment later a young woman with dramatic eyes and a long, curly brown ponytail approached her. "Are you Michelle Tanner?" she asked in a friendly voice.

"Yes, I'm Michelle. Are you the makeover person?"

The woman nodded. "I'm Joanne. Ready to get started?"

"Sure," Michelle said.

First Joanne stared at her with her head tilted to one side. "Wow!" she exclaimed. The makeup artist took a strand of Michelle's hair between her fingers. "Your hair is fantastic!" she told her. "And your skin is wonderful. I'll just dab on a little blusher, and that's it."

Michelle frowned. "But I want to try some makeup. Put a lot on!"

Joanne laughed. "Okay, Michelle. I'll see what I can do." Michelle smiled as Joanne leaned closer with an eyebrow brush, but then she saw something that made the smile on her face freeze.

## And the Winner Is . . .

Mrs. Cruz was standing right behind Joanne!

"Michelle," Mrs. Cruz said. "What are you doing here? I thought you were sick."

Joanne didn't seem to notice Mrs. Cruz. "Don't move a muscle, okay, sweetie?" she told Michelle. "I'll be right back with some colors I want to try on your eyes."

Michelle scrunched her eyes shut. *Please let this just be a nightmare,* she thought. She opened her eyes again. Mrs. Cruz was still standing right in front of her, looking really disappointed.

"I'm sorry," Michelle whispered. She wished that the earth would open up and swallow her up right then and there.

"I thought you were responsible," Mrs. Cruz told her. "That's why I gave you the money early. I think I'm going to have to go to your father about this."

"No, please, Mrs. Cruz," Michelle said. She knew she had to explain everything. "I have to—"

"Unless . . ." Mrs. Cruz interrupted her. "Maybe the best thing would be for you to

**113**

come to the restaurant bright and early to-morrow morning to make up the time you've missed today. That way we won't have to say a thing about this to your father. All right?" Mrs. Cruz said.

"*Tomorrow?*" Michelle echoed. "But—"

Mrs. Cruz didn't let Michelle finish. "That's right, dear. *Tomorrow.*" She patted her on the arm and then hurried off toward the food court.

Michelle slumped down on her stool. But tomorrow is the fashion show, she thought.

# Chapter
## 13

Stephanie woke with a start on Saturday morning. "I forgot the dresses in the washing machine!"

She sat up and shoved her feet into her slippers. Michelle's bed was already empty. Stephanie smiled. She must be really excited about the fashion show, she thought as she bounded downstairs.

"Morning, Steph," Uncle Jesse said. He looked up from his cup of coffee. "You must be psyched for your big fashion show."

"Yup. Be right back," Stephanie told him. She was already heading for the door. "I have

**115**

to put the dresses in the dryer so they're ready in time."

She hurried to the laundry room. Opening the lid of the washing machine, she pulled out a clump of blotchy blue and green fabric. This dress doesn't look so good, Stephanie thought with a sigh. The colors must have run when I washed it.

She shook it out. But something else was wrong, too. One of the sleeves was dangling loosely from the shoulder.

"Uh-oh," she muttered. "Looks like I didn't glue that one on tight enough."

As she smoothed out the dress for a better look, the sleeve came completely loose and fell to the floor!

"Oh, no!" Stephanie cried when the other sleeve pulled away from the dress and fell off, too. Then the main seams separated and the body of the dress came apart into two large, flat pieces.

Stephanie was left holding the front of the dress and nothing else. "This *can't* be happening!" she wailed.

Joey popped his head into the laundry

room. "Something the matter, Steph?" he asked with a yawn.

Stephanie held up the pieces of her dress. "Does *this* answer your question?" She bit down on her lip. The last thing she wanted to do was start crying. "The fashion show starts in less than an hour and a half, and our dresses are ruined!" she told him. "They fell apart in the wash."

Joey poked at the fabric and frowned. "That's weird," he said. "I may not know much about sewing, but I really don't think that's supposed to happen."

"No kidding." Stephanie ran a hand through her hair. "Actually, now that you mention it, I didn't exactly sew them. But I used Super Glue, and that's supposed to hold anything, right?"

"Super Glue?" Joey scratched his chin.

"Right," Stephanie said. "It was D.J.'s idea. I found a whole tube of the stuff in the tool-box. I should sue them for false advertising. For ruining my life. For—"

"In the toolbox?" he interrupted. He had a weird look on his face. "You mean the glue in the purple tube?"

"That's the stuff." Stephanie nodded. "It's a total cheat! I mean, I've seen those Super Glue ads on TV, and they all say it'll hold practically anything."

Joey turned and hurried off without another word. A moment later he reappeared with the familiar-looking purple tube in his hand. "Take a closer look."

Stephanie didn't know what he was talking about, but she took the tube and peered at it. After a moment, she gasped. "Wait a minute," she said. "This doesn't say Super Glue. It says Superbo-Glue. What's Superbo-Glue?"

Joey grinned weakly. "Well, this is just a theory. But I'd say that it's a cheap imitation of Super Glue and that it doesn't work very well."

Stephanie sighed. "But the contest is in a few hours. What am I supposed to do?"

Joey shrugged. "Sorry, Steph," he said. "Looks like you'll have to find something else to wear."

"Where's Michelle?" Stephanie moaned. She headed for the stairs. "We need to come up with an alternate plan. Fast."

"Wait!" Joey hurried after her. "Michelle's

not home. I just dropped her off at the mall."

Stephanie stopped. "Really?" she said. Her heart was sinking. "I guess that means I'm on my own."

She raced for the stairs even though she felt sick to her stomach. Could this morning be any more horrid? She was supposed to leave for the mall in less than an hour. How was she going to find something fabulous to wear before then? And how was she going to tell Michelle that she'd ruined their beautiful dresses?

Stephanie rummaged through her closet frantically. She was looking for something— anything—she could wear in the contest. But nothing seemed right. All her clothes were or-dinary, boring, wrong! If only she hadn't re-turned those dresses from Zoom!

She hurried to D.J.'s room. Come on, D.J., Stephanie thought. You've got to have some-thing perfect that I can borrow.

But D.J. wasn't there, and Stephanie didn't dare borrow anything without asking. Even in an emergency.

Suddenly, Stephanie remembered that Aunt

Becky was about her size. Close enough, anyway, she thought. She took the steps to the third floor two at a time.

"Hi," she said, bursting into her aunt and uncle's apartment. Becky sat on the floor, helping the twins build a house out of blocks.

"Stephanie!" Nicky and Alex cried in unison. They jumped up and ran toward her.

"Hey, guys." Stephanie stooped down long enough to give each of her little cousins a quick hug. "Sorry, no time to play now."

"What's up, Steph?" Aunt Becky asked.

Stephanie quickly explained her problem. "So I thought maybe you had something cool I could wear," she finished. "You know, some one-of-a-kind designer original, an old ball gown, whatever."

Aunt Becky smiled. "I don't know about a ball gown," she said. "But you're welcome to borrow anything you like. I think my dresses will probably all be a little big for Michelle, though."

"Michelle!" Stephanie groaned. "I almost forgot I have to find an outfit for her to wear, too." Stephanie slumped against the wall. It was hopeless.

"Thanks anyway," she told her aunt. "I guess it's time to move on to Plan C. I just have to figure out what Plan C is."

"Good luck," Aunt Becky said. "And, Stephanie, no matter what you end up wearing today, you know we'll all be there in the audience, cheering you on."

"Thanks," Stephanie said again. She headed back downstairs to her own room. She gazed into her closet. Her mind was racing. She needed a last-minute inspiration—a brilliant one.

I almost turned some old upholstery fabric into a pair of awesome dresses, she thought. I just have to figure out another creative solution. She checked her watch. In the next forty-seven minutes.

"Maybe I could wear a toga," she muttered, grabbing her favorite sheet off of her bed. She draped it around herself, glanced in the mirror, and sighed. She looked ridiculous.

She checked her watch again. Forty-four minutes. She was running out of time, and fast. If she didn't find something to wear soon, she would end up at the fashion show in the pajamas she still had on.

Danny poked his head into the room a few minutes later. "Better get dressed, Steph," he said. "We've got to leave soon if you want to get to the mall on time."

"What's the point?" Stephanie threw her hands up in the air. "Didn't Joey tell you? The dresses are ruined!"

Danny nodded. "Joey told me," he said. "I'm sorry, Steph. I know you're disappointed, especially after all the hard work you put into them. But I'm sure you can find something else to wear."

Stephanie shook her head sadly. "Guess again. I can't find a single thing in this whole house!"

"Oh, come on." Danny walked over to her closet and started poking around inside. "Here you go," he said. "What about this? This looks terrific on you."

Stephanie saw that he was holding her embroidered peasant dress. She bought it last year when her family went to Mexico.

"Hmm." Stephanie put her hands on her hips and stared at the dress. "I forgot about that. I guess I didn't notice it when I was looking through the closet before."

## And the Winner Is . . .

"You always said that you loved this dress," Danny reminded her. "And Michelle has one almost like it, remember?" He dug around in the closet for a second and then brought out a similar dress in a smaller size. "So you two can still match!"

"Well . . ." Stephanie hesitated. The two dresses weren't exactly high fashion. But they were nice, and she knew they looked good on her and Michelle. Better yet, they were there.

"So, are you going to wear these dresses?" Danny asked.

Stephanie made up her mind. She took the larger dress from her father. "They'll have to do," she told him. "I'll be down in a second. Could you put Michelle's in a bag or something? She'll have to change at the mall."

"Sure thing," her father said, and left the room.

Stephanie stared at the dress dangling limply on the hanger. She thought about the high-fashion silver and bronze dresses that Rhonda and Rianne were going to wear and sighed. "I just hope the judges don't laugh us off the stage." Stephanie sighed.

# MICHELLE

## Chapter
## 14

"Do you know when Mrs. Cruz is getting here?" Michelle asked Charlie. "I need to ask her something."

Charlie shrugged. "I'm really not sure," he replied. "She has a meeting across town and said she didn't know what time it would be finished. Is it something I can help you with?"

"No, I don't think so," Michelle said. "Thanks anyway."

She bit her lip and glanced at her watch as Charlie walked toward the front of the taco stand. So much for my big plan, she thought. Even after what I did yesterday, I'm sure I could still explain things to Mrs. Cruz. If she knew how important this fashion show is, I'm sure she'd let me make up my work another time. She shook her head in frustration. But I can't explain anything to her if she's not here!

Michelle walked over and checked the list of tasks on the desk. She was trying not to imagine how surprised and upset Stephanie would be when her modeling partner didn't show up.

Still, what could Michelle do? She couldn't leave without getting permission from Mrs. Cruz no matter how much she wanted to. Not after pretending to be sick yesterday. Not after Mrs. Cruz had already paid her.

Maybe she'll get here soon, Michelle thought, sneaking another peek at her watch. She was trying to keep her hopes up, but she was running out of time. The fashion show was supposed to start in fifteen minutes.

Twenty minutes later, Michelle heard Mrs. Cruz sing out a greeting from the front of the taco stand. Michelle dropped the dishrags she was folding and rushed out front.

"Hello, dear," Mrs. Cruz said. "Working hard?"

"Sure," Michelle answered. "But listen, Mrs. Cruz, there's something I need to ask you about."

"All right, dear." Mrs. Cruz hurried past her to the back, where she grabbed her apron off its hook. "But just one moment, okay? I want to show you something first."

"Um, actually, it's kind of . . ." Michelle began.

But John interrupted her. He hurried up to Mrs. Cruz. "I'm glad you're here, boss," he exclaimed. "The napkin supplier called with a question about the last invoice. He wants you to call him back right away."

"I'd better take care of this," Mrs. Cruz decided. "I'll be with you in a moment, Michelle." Mrs. Cruz picked up the phone and dialed a number.

Michelle could feel the minutes ticking past as Mrs. Cruz chatted with the napkin supplier. The phone call seemed to take forever. But finally, Mrs. Cruz said good-bye and hung up.

"Mrs. Cruz . . ." Michelle began again.

Mrs. Cruz held up a finger. "Wait there, Michelle," she said. "I'll be right back."

Michelle didn't know what to do. All she needed was a minute to explain things to her boss. But Mrs. Cruz was too busy.

A moment later, Mrs. Cruz reappeared, holding a large garment bag and smiling more brightly than ever. "I have a very special job for you today," Mrs. Cruz began.

"That's great, Mrs. Cruz," Michelle said. "But first, I really need to ask you—"

"Get ready to have some fun!" Mrs. Cruz sang out. It was as if she hadn't even heard Michelle. With a flourish, she pulled out a strange-looking outfit.

Michelle blinked in surprise. Her boss was holding up a short black jacket trimmed with gold thread, along with a pair of shiny black pants and a bright red shirt. A short black wig and a pair of black tights hung off a hook at the side of the hanger. It all looked like something that a young Mexican boy in an old movie might wear.

"That's a cute costume," Michelle said. "But—"

"I'm glad you like it, dear." Mrs. Cruz flipped the jacket around to show Michelle the back. A dancing taco was embroidered underneath the restaurant's name. "Because I want you to be my walking advertisement!" Mrs. Cruz continued. "Now hurry and put it on—we have to get you right out there soon, while people are deciding where to eat lunch."

Michelle felt her heart sink all the way to her feet. Mrs. Cruz looked so excited about her idea. How was Michelle ever going to get out of this one?

She stole a peek at the clock on the wall and saw that it was even later than she thought—almost twenty minutes past the starting time of the fashion show. I probably already missed the whole thing! Michelle thought. She blinked back some tears. I can't believe I let down Stephanie, *again*! She'll never forgive me!

Michelle stared at the Mexican costume in Mrs. Cruz's hands. She had already disappointed her sister. She couldn't disappoint Mrs. Cruz again, as well. "Okay." Michelle reached to take the costume from Mrs. Cruz. "I'll go get changed."

She walked to the rest room, her feet dragging the whole way. Michelle felt awful, but she changed out of her regular clothes and put on the costume. She straightened the collar of the red shirt and tucked her blond hair beneath the dark wig, then returned to the kitchen.

"You look wonderful, dear!" Mrs. Cruz sounded so happy that Michelle felt a teensy bit better. "But I almost forgot the finishing touch. Wait right here, dear. I'll be back."

Mrs. Cruz returned a moment later carrying an enormous sombrero. Tiny plastic tacos dangled all around the edge of the huge hat. It was so silly-looking that Michelle almost giggled.

"Here you go, dear," Mrs. Cruz said. She set the sombrero on top of Michelle's wig. "That puts the perfect touch on it. Now take a stack of the advertising fliers from the desk drawer. You can hand them out to people while you walk around the mall."

"Okay." Michelle walked over to the desk and grabbed a handful of the brightly printed fliers. They featured the same dancing-taco logo as the back of her jacket, along with coupons for half-price burritos and enchiladas.

"You'll do fine, dear," Mrs. Cruz promised. She patted Michelle on the shoulder. "Just have fun with it."

I wish I could, Michelle thought. But she couldn't stop thinking about how she had humiliated Stephanie—leaving her without a partner for the fashion show.

Maybe I should talk to Mrs. Cruz about this, Michelle thought. I really should go apologize to Stephanie.

"Attention please . . ." An announcement sounded across the mall. "Paging Michelle Tanner. Michelle Tanner, please meet your sister at the fountain plaza immediately."

Michelle's eyes widened. Was the sombrero cutting off the circulation to her ears, or did she really just hear the announcer calling her name?

"Oh, dear," Mrs. Cruz told Michelle. "You'd better go see what that's all about. I just hope nothing is wrong."

**And the Winner Is . . .**

For a second, Michelle was worried, too. But then she realized that Stephanie was paging her to come to the fashion show. Did that mean it wasn't too late after all?

Michelle didn't have a second to waste. "Thanks, Mrs. Cruz," she said. "I'll be back soon!"

Not even bothering to remove her sombrero, Michelle took off for the fountain. If she ran the whole way, she just might get there in time.

# Chapter
# 15

"Please tell me Michelle's going to be here," Stephanie said, standing by the stage at the fountain plaza. She stared at the bag with Michelle's peasant dress inside as if it could somehow grant her wish. "Please tell me she's not going to disappear again for no good reason."

"She won't," Allie assured her. "I'm sure she won't."

"She had to have heard your page," Darcy added. "Michelle will be here any second."

Stephanie wasn't convinced. This day was turning out to be a total disaster—from the disintegrating dresses to the missing sister. She glanced into the audience. The rows of folding chairs were nearly filled. Her entire family was seated in the second row. Even her five-year-old cousins, Nicky and Alex, were there.

"Come on," Stephanie told her friends. "I guess I should at least check in with hair and makeup."

They walked around to the back of the stage, where Joanne was brushing blush on Rhonda. Rianne stood beside them, gazing at her reflection in a mirror. She caught sight of Stephanie.

"Wow, Stephanie," Rianne called out. "You look fantastic!"

"Thanks." Stephanie forced herself to smile, even though she didn't much feel like it.

Joanne finished with Rhonda. "Have a seat, Stephanie," the makeup artist said. "Your Mexican dress is adorable! And I know just what to do with your hair. We'll sweep it up onto your head and hold it with these Mexican combs." She pulled two silver combs set with turquoise from her accessory box.

"Plus . . . a little bit of blush and eye shadow, a dab of lip gloss—and you'll be all set!"

"Thanks, Joanne." Stephanie glanced at her reflection in the mirror. "I guess I do look okay," she said to Darcy and Allie. "Still, this definitely isn't how I imagined this day turning out. I really wanted to knock everybody off their feet with our cool, totally original psychedelic dresses."

"I know," Allie said. "But everyone will love what you're wearing now, too."

Stephanie sighed. She straightened her flowing skirt and checked her watch again. "I hope I get a chance to find out," she said, "because if Michelle doesn't show up, I won't even get to go onstage." She put her head in her hands. "I can't believe she's letting me down like this. I hope whatever she's doing right now is worth it, because I'm never talking to her again."

Stephanie jumped as a microphone at the side of the stage crackled to life. She glanced over at the stage.

"Welcome, fashion fans," Ms. Nolan said into the microphone. "It's almost time for the start of San Francisco's Most Fabulous Sisters

Modeling Contest! But first I would like to introduce the sisters who made this all possible—Fiona and Felicia Miarra!"

Stephanie felt a few butterflies in her stomach when she spotted the two slender women in the front row. They were wearing the most outrageous outfits she'd ever seen. Felicia shimmered in a silk suit with a blue and green wave pattern, and an exotic purple cape. Fiona wore a fuchsia minidress with big gold buttons, and a sailor hat, and carried a purse shaped just like the *Titanic.* They are so cool, Stephanie thought.

"I know that we're a little behind schedule, but sit tight a few more minutes," Ms. Nolan went on. "We'll be starting in about ten minutes."

"Hey, Steph," Darcy whispered. "Want us to do one last search for Michelle?"

Stephanie thought fast and pointed to Allie. "You wait here, okay? If Michelle shows up, make her put this on." She gave the bag containing Michelle's dress to her friend. "And don't let her out of your sight until I get back." She spun to point at Darcy. "You take the west side of the mall. I'll go east. We'll meet back here asap."

Allie looked worried. "You'd better move fast. They're going to start soon."

"Don't worry," Stephanie told her. "Yesterday after the makeover, they told us we're going in alphabetical order. So we still have a little while before they get to Tanner."

She and Darcy hurried away in opposite directions. Stephanie made her way down the east aisle of the mall. She glanced into every store she passed and scanned the faces of all the shoppers. Michelle was nowhere to be found.

This is hopeless, Stephanie thought after a while. I'm never going to find Michelle. This mall's just too big and too crowded!

Stephanie felt like sitting down in the middle of the aisle and crying. Still, she kept searching until she heard another announcement over the loudspeaker system. "Attention, shoppers, the Miarra San Francisco's Most Fabulous Sisters Modeling Contest is beginning now at the fountain plaza. Don't miss this special event featuring San Francisco's most fabulous sisters!"

## And the Winner Is . . .

Stephanie forced herself to go to the end of the aisle. Then she turned back with a sigh. It was time to give up. She could only go back to the fashion show and hope that Michelle would be there.

She found Darcy and Allie waiting for her at the plaza. "No luck," Darcy reported in a glum voice.

Allie nodded toward the stage, where two blond girls walked and twirled. "Those are the Gifford sisters," she told Stephanie. "I think there are still at least six or seven more pairs before they get to you."

Stephanie nodded. "I've never been so glad that my last name is Tanner. Michelle and I are the last ones to go onstage."

She and her friends watched the Giffords finish. The audience clapped like crazy. Next, a pair of very tall girls stepped onstage in matching long black skirts, white blouses, and silver hoop earrings. Then came a pair of sisters who looked nothing alike. Stephanie noticed that one of them wore the very same T-shirt dress she returned to Zoom.

After that it was Rianne and Rhonda's turn.

The two of them were dressed in their high-fashion outfits from Verve.

"Wow," Darcy said. "Those dresses are gorgeous. And the hair-and-makeup people did a really great job on them."

"They look totally—professional." Allie added.

Stephanie knew that her friends were right. She checked her watch once more. If her sister was going to show up at all, it would have to be soon.

"Stephanie!" a breathless voice exclaimed from behind them.

Stephanie whirled around, weak with relief. "Michelle!" she cried. "It's about time you showed . . ." Her voice trailed off and she stared at her younger sister in disbelief. "What are you wearing?"

Michelle pushed back the giant sombrero on her head and glanced down at her own outfit. "Oh, this?" she said. "Um, well, you see . . ."

Michelle seemed to be having trouble figuring out how to explain herself, and Stephanie didn't have time to wait. She glanced at the stage, where Rianne and Rhonda were just stepping down after their turn. A pair of red-headed girls in white dresses took their place.

"I think their last name is Summers," Stephanie whispered. That means we're probably next!"

She grabbed the clothes bag back from Allie and quickly pulled out Michelle's peasant dress. "Here!" She shoved the dress toward her sister. "Quick. Put this on," she told Michelle. "We'll stand in front of you so no one will see."

"Stephanie! She can't change right here in the middle of the mall," Allie insisted.

Michelle grabbed the dress. "What's this? Where are our special dresses?"

"Don't ask," Stephanie muttered.

Darcy gazed toward the judges' table. "Uh-oh. I think they're about to call your—"

"Tanner!" Ms. Nolan called over the microphone. "May we have our next contestants, please. Stephanie and Michelle Tanner."

Stephanie's heart skipped a beat. This was a disaster. A total and complete disaster!

"Come on," Michelle said, already heading toward the stage. "That's us."

"Wait!" Stephanie cried. Suddenly being disqualified didn't seem like such a terrible thing. Michelle couldn't go onstage wearing that ridiculous Mexican costume. No way. She would be laughed out of the city—and so would Stephanie!

Stephanie grabbed for Michelle's arm. She had to stop her before she made fools of them both. But Michelle was already out of reach.

"Tell me this isn't happening!" Stephanie moaned. But it was. Michelle, dressed in that ridiculous outfit, pushed her way through the crowd and up onto the stage.

# Chapter
# 16

I didn't let Stephanie down! Michelle thought as she ran cheerfully onto the stage. All the sneaking around to keep her secret from Stephanie was worth it. Michelle had bought her sister a cool birthday present, and she had made it to the fashion show, too.

A low murmur echoed through the audience when Michelle pranced down the runway. That made her a little nervous. Am I not walking like a model? she wondered.

Then Michelle caught sight of two weird-looking ladies with big smiles on their faces in the audience. One was wearing a sailor hat and holding a big purse that was shaped like a steamship. The other had on a suit covered with blue and green waves that looked like the ocean, and a dramatic purple cape thrown over one shoulder. Michelle couldn't help giggling. Boy, did they look stupid! Why are they dressed like that to come to the mall? she wondered.

"Michelle!" Stephanie whispered from behind her.

She glanced over her shoulder at Stephanie, who was just climbing onstage. Stephanie covered her face with one hand, and her cheeks were bright pink.

Suddenly, Michelle remembered what she was wearing—the El Taco Loco costume. Michelle gasped. She lifted her hand to straighten her sombrero and hit one of the hanging plastic tacos. It swung back and forth in front of her face.

A flush of embarrassment crept over her cheeks when Michelle reached the end of the runway. Even worse, the two strangely dressed women were whispering and pointing at her.

## And the Winner Is . . .

Michelle gulped. They're all laughing at me, she thought. And they're probably laughing at Stephanie, too. I ruined everything for her. Stephanie will probably never talk to me again! She quickly turned to go back down the runway.

Then the woman with the steamship purse stood up and screamed. "Stop!" She pointed at Michelle. "Stop everything!"

# Chapter
# 17

How humiliating! Stephanie thought as she watched Michelle in her Mexican costume. I bet Fiona and Felicia think I'm making fun of their fashion show. They must hate me!

She wanted to tell the Miarra sisters that she had nothing to do with Michelle's silly costume, but she couldn't get the words out.

Stephanie watched in horror as the two designers whispered to each other. A moment later Fiona began to applaud. Felicia soon joined in.

"Huh?" Stephanie said under her breath. "They *like* it?"

"Brava!" the woman in the wave suit cried, rolling the *R* dramatically. "Wonderful! Stupendous!"

"Fantastic!" the other woman added. "Incredible! Simply marvelous!"

Seconds later, the entire audience started to clap along with the two women.

Stephanie made her way to the front of the runway and stood beside Michelle as the applause continued. "Are they kidding?" she murmured just loud enough for Michelle to hear.

But Fiona and Felicia didn't seem to be joking. They stepped toward the stage, still clapping loudly. "Please, may we have a closer look, girls?" Fiona asked.

Felicia nodded. "And please, could you tell us your names again?"

Stephanie took a nervous step forward. "I'm Stephanie Tanner," she said. "And this is my little sister, Michelle."

"Nice to meet you," Michelle added.

"The pleasure is all ours," the woman in the fuchsia outfit said. "I am Fiona Miarra—"

"I am Felicia Miarra," the other woman

**1 4 5**

added. "And my sister is correct. The pleasure is entirely ours. We've never seen such young girls with such an original, unique—"

"Completely creative sense of style," Fiona finished for her sister. "We're stunned. We're amazed."

"We absolutely love your look!" Felicia declared. "It's so fresh, so new—"

"So happening," Fiona broke in, nodding in agreement.

"You two girls are at the forefront of a fashion revolution!" Felicia said. "You're visionaries. You're—"

"Trendsetters," Fiona put in. "How did you know that this was where fashion was headed?"

Stephanie wasn't sure how to respond. The Mexican costume was all a big mistake. She wasn't even sure why Michelle was wearing it.

Michelle peeked at Stephanie. "Um, I'm not sure," she told the Miarra sisters.

Stephanie grabbed Michelle's sombrero and plopped it on her own head. She put her arm around her little sister and squeezed. "I guess we're just lucky that way."

## And the Winner Is . . .

"Please,"—Fiona bowed and gestured toward the stage—"you two must have your triumphant walk down the runway."

Stephanie and Michelle exchanged a look. Then Michelle took Stephanie's hand and proudly strode down the stage.

"Thanks for making my day totally awesome, Michelle," Stephanie told her as they showed off their outfits. She pulled off the sombrero and placed it back on Michelle's head.

The audience clapped as if they would never stop. Stephanie and Michelle waved at their family, who was hooting and cheering.

Stephanie was in shock when they stepped off the stage. She couldn't believe what had just happened. Did she just dream it—or did Fiona and Felicia Miarra really love their look?

No, it was all too weird. I *must* be imagining it, she decided as she and Michelle gathered at the edge of the stage with the rest of the contestants.

"Okay, now we come to the moment you've all been waiting for," Ms. Nolan said into the microphone. "I'd like to invite our chief judges onto the stage to announce the winning sisters. Please welcome world-famous fashion designers Fiona and Felicia Miarra!"

The audience cheered wildly as the stylish sisters climbed onto the stage. Stephanie crossed her fingers and held her breath.

Fiona cleared her throat and smiled. "It's time to announce our winners. I want to congratulate all of the sisters who entered today. You were all very stylish, very beautiful, very professional—"

"And very wonderful," Felicia continued. "You can be proud of yourselves. But I must admit one pair of sisters here today stood out among all the rest. These two young ladies have so much personal style, so much confidence—"

Fiona nodded in agreement. "So much presence on the runway. They truly deserve the title of San Francisco's Most Fabulous Sisters. And those sisters are Stephanie—"

"And Michelle Tanner!" Felicia finished. "Please, come up here, girls!"

Stephanie still couldn't believe that this was

happening. She could feel herself grinning from ear to ear.

"We won!" Michelle cried. "Come on, let's get up there! We won!"

They climbed the steps onto the stage and walked over to the Miarras. Waves of applause washed over them. Stephanie wasn't sure, but she thought she heard Joey whooping, even over all the other noise. She looked out at her family and saw them all standing and clapping. She smiled and waved. Then she spotted Darcy and Allie cheering her on from the side of the stage. Stephanie waved at them, too.

She turned as Fiona handed her an ivory-colored envelope with a gold seal. "For you, Stephanie," she said. Felicia handed an identical envelope to Michelle.

Stephanie peeked inside hers. It held special gift certificates for a shopping spree at Verve, the Miarra boutique, and three other designer stores. Then Stephanie pulled out a special invitation to join Felicia and Fiona for dinner at Pacific Rim.

She remembered all the trouble she had

gone through to get the grand prize—cutting the rug, breaking the sewing machine, ruining the dresses . . .

It was all worth it, she said to herself. Every single bit of it.

"Thank you!" Stephanie said. "This is fantastic!"

Beside her, Michelle bounced with excitement. "This is the best!" she said. "The best day ever!"

Stephanie and Michelle soon found themselves surrounded by family and friends. Allie and Darcy reached them first and smothered Stephanie in a huge hug. Right behind them, Stephanie saw her father, D.J., Joey, Uncle Jesse, Aunt Becky, and the twins. Michelle's two best friends were rushing toward them from the other direction.

This has to be a dream, Stephanie thought happily as Uncle Jesse grabbed her in a big bear hug while the twins cheered, Joey traded a high-five with Michelle, and Danny told everyone in earshot that Stephanie and Michelle were his daughters.

Stephanie glanced at Michelle jumping up

and down in her silly sombrero. Then she took another peek at the invitation to dinner with the Miarras. Well, if this *is* a dream, she thought smiling, I hope I don't have to wake up!

Later that afternoon, Stephanie sat on the couch, flipping through a magazine and thinking about all the events of the past week. Michelle skipped into the living room and flopped onto the couch beside her.

"Next contest we enter, Michelle," Stephanie said with a laugh, "I'm not letting you out of my sight. That way, you'll never ever be late!"

"That's what I wanted to talk to you about," Michelle admitted, and held out a long velvet box. "This is why I was late all the time."

"What's in there?" Stephanie asked.

"It's for you." Michelle handed her the box. "Sorry I didn't have time to wrap it. Happy birthday!"

"But my birthday's not until next Friday," Stephanie said in surprise.

"I know," Michelle said. "But I couldn't wait to give it to you. So open it!"

Stephanie lifted the lid of the box—and found a delicate silver bracelet nestled inside. "Wow!" she cried. "It's that bracelet I wanted! It's beautiful! Oh, Michelle, thank you!"

She gave her sister a puzzled look. "But how does this explain your being late all the time?"

Michelle looked a little shy. "I wanted to get you something special this year, all by my-self," she told her. "And I knew that you liked the bracelet . . . so I worked with Mrs. Cruz at El Taco Loco all week to earn the money."

"Really? You got a job just for me?" Steph-anie was touched.

Michelle nodded. "That's why I was late all those times. I couldn't get away from my job."

"That's amazing!" Stephanie cried. "I can't believe you had a job all week and I didn't even know!"

"Anyway," Michelle went on, "I'm really sorry for making you worry when I didn't show up."

"That's okay." Stephanie held out her arm. "Will you put the bracelet on me?" she asked. She held still as Michelle carefully fastened the bracelet around her wrist, then Stephanie held up her arm and watched the slender silver band catch the light.

She loved the bracelet because it was beautiful, but she loved it even more knowing what Michelle did to get it for her. It made it even more special. She leaned over and gave Michelle a big hug. "You know, as sisters go, you're all right."

"Thanks," Michelle replied, hugging her back. "You're not so bad yourself."

"That's what I like to see," Danny said, walking into the living room. "San Francisco's most fabulous sisters hugging each other."

"Let's not get mushy, Dad," Michelle replied.

"Okay, okay," Danny said, holding up his hands. "But will you two be even more fabulous and help me put the furniture back where it was? I think I like it better that way."

Stephanie gasped. They couldn't move the furniture. She hadn't told Dad about the cut in the rug yet! She glanced at her father. "I have to show you something first." Stephanie jumped off the couch and pushed the sofa off the area rug. "I kind of had an accident with the utility knife," she said meekly. "I glued it back together."

"Why didn't you tell me sooner?" Danny stared at the rug, then slowly moved his gaze to Stephanie. "What do you have to say for yourself, Stephanie?"

"I'm sorry I didn't tell you about it," Stephanie admitted. "And I'll pay for a new rug, I promise. I'll get a job. I'll do anything!"

Michelle pulled at Stephanie's sleeve. "I can put in a good word for you at El Taco Loco." She grinned. "You'll get to wear a really fashionable costume."

Stephanie put her arm around her sister and smiled at Danny. "Is she a fabulous sister, or what?"

# A brand-new series
## starring
## Stephanie AND Michelle!

# FULL HOUSE™
# SISTERS

## When sisters get together...
## expect the unexpected!

A MINSTREL® BOOK
Published by Pocket Books

# FULL HOUSE™
# Michelle

A MINSTREL® BOOK
Published by Pocket Books